The Third Secret

By

Sarah Jane Gross

Original Artwork by Sarah Jane Gross

Author's Note:

While this book is largely fictitious,
I do pay tribute to family members
long gone, who we loved and cherished.

Table of Contents

The sea-storm breeze whispers and whines
When the sky is not clear in May,
Where a kaleidoscopic pool ripples and shines
And she sits in the copse with paper in hand,
And she sits and she dreams all day.
She waits for a sign from the bird or the tree.
It is not for someone but something much greater,
With a sigh she says, "come here to me",
And she hears the breeze sing now, "be patient, dear—
later."

-May Bell Sebastian, 1896.

Chapter 1

At the Train Station

Coos County, Oregon, November 1920

It was a cool and cloudy day in Coos County, Oregon. A thin layer of fog hung in the air, and the streets were damp from the morning rain. Seagulls circled in the sky above the ships docked in the pier and preparing to make sail with exports of lumber. Work in the lumbermill and the neighboring shipyard continued on, as busy as ever. The buzz of activity could be felt straight through to the train station in North Bend, which bustled at the noon hour as dozens filled the depot to wait for the next passenger line to arrive.

Betty Featherwin pushed back the sleeve of her coat to check the time on her watch.

"It's expected at a quarter past, isn't it?" The woman standing to her right—Ms. Elizabeth Satton, executive assistant at the bookshop, The Sapphire Key—asked.

Betty nodded, and pulled her coat more snugly around her as the cold Oregon mist, common in these late autumn days, gave the air an added chill. She had closed her bookshop during the lunch hour while she and Elizabeth had ventured down to the station—along with their friends Edith and Samuel—to await the train.

For a young woman of 21, she was accomplished and somewhat older in spirit than her age would suggest. She had inherited The Sapphire Key from her father and worked tirelessly to make a success of it. After running it on her own for a couple of years, she hired Elizabeth Satton part-time, and then full-time, to assist her in the management of the shop. It had become a staple in the coastal town of Marshfield, and with each year, it seemed to grow and become more profitable. This pleased Betty greatly, for she wished for nothing more than to make her late father, Henry, proud and to honor his memory. The Sapphire Key had meant the world to him, and now, to her, the shop was like her second home.

In the recent months, she had spent a great deal of time at the shop and consequently saw an increase in customers and sales. This was partly due to hard work, and partly due to fortuitous circumstances. A large orange cat, who was friendly and communicative, had come into her shop and made itself at home there. This cat—Leopold—was beloved by all and was truly a part of the Featherwin family. He was also a sort of protector of The Sapphire Key. In fact, he was there now, curled up on the blue entryway rug to guard the shop until Betty and Elizabeth returned.

In addition to meeting Leopold, Betty had made the acquaintance of Mr. Thomas Erwinshire, a publisher from Dayton, Washington, who owned a publishing and editing business, Erwinshire Publishing. He had sought out The Sapphire Key as a potential distributor for a new manuscript. This turn of events had worked in his favor, and in Betty's. She found a new business partner in Thomas with the book deal, and unexpectedly found a new friend in him as well. They had connected over a poem by May Bell Sebastian, a mysterious and talented poet who also happened to be Thomas' deceased mother. Thomas had lost both of his parents before he was a year old, and had always wanted to learn more about them. In a string of events that eventually led Betty and Thomas to a photograph of May Bell Sebastian, dated 1890, they had slowly begun to learn more about this woman and her past. They were still far from having all of the answers, however. Betty had promised to help Thomas in his search.

It was Thomas who they were waiting for now. He had returned to his office in Washington for a few days to catch up on some work and square things with his associate. The associate, Mr. John Noble, preferred the traveling aspect of his job much more than staying in the office. In a gesture of real restraint, John had agreed to stay put and manage the office while Thomas remained in Coos County for longer than originally intended. Thomas' goal in returning was—in addition to checking in on existing projects—negotiating with John over his schedule and, hopefully, allotting himself a couple of weeks' more time in Coos County.

Betty glanced over the crowd. Still no sign of his train yet. She wondered if he had managed to persuade his associate to hold down the fort a little longer. It would be a stretch, to say the least, but somehow, she felt sure that Thomas had been able to manage it. At least, she surely *hoped* he did. She rather enjoyed his company, and others in town liked him as well. They all would not mind if he stayed. He was a friend of the respected Highley and Ball families, after all. This, coupled with his good breeding and amiable nature, turned him into a "local" faster than other "outsiders" who came into town. Betty did not wish to see him leave yet, especially as their search for information about Thomas' mother was far from over (as Betty had reminded him before he left).

She had not expected the train station to be quite so busy, but then again, with more and more people using the railway, it was not much of a surprise. The Spokane, Portland, and Seattle Railway was a profitable industry. In fact, many of the men she knew worked on the railroad in some capacity, if they did not work at the lumbermill.

"Thank you for driving us, Samuel," Betty said, turning

to the man on her left.

The man, Samuel Clarkson, merely lowered the brim of his hat in a gesture of acknowledgment. He worked as lead engineer at the lumbermill, and made a good living doing so. He did not have to do this work, as he came from a fairly well-to-do family in upper North Bend. He felt, nonetheless, that he ought to earn his living, not simply be handed it, which was indeed a mark of his good character. Still, growing up around the well-to-do, he could easily spot a woman of good breeding by her speech and dress. Admittedly, he had always been attracted to this type of woman when it came to settling down and raising a family. This explains why he fell in love so quickly with Ms. Edith Smithson. The first moment Samuel spotted Edith in the mess hall at the lumbermill, chatting away in her singsong voice and dressed to the nines in an outfit she had recently purchased downtown, he was smitten. After just a couple of months of courtship, Samuel proposed to Edith. Now, with a ring on her left hand, Edith was the happiest woman of all.

At first, Betty could not understand how Edith and Samuel got along so well. Edith—her bubbly, young friend Edith, who preferred gossip, shopping, and socializing—was now settled and married. Samuel, this hardworking engineer, seemed to have an excess of patience and seemed to dote on his new wife. Edith was always wearing a new hat, gloves, or dress, and often talked of visiting Samuel's "splendid" relatives.

Despite their outward differences, they just *worked* when they were together. Samuel's evenness balanced out Edith's bubbliness. Edith enjoying lunching with him at the lumbermill; he enjoyed dancing with her at the music hall. Edith's mother, Ruth, applauded Edith on making a sensible match. Samuel's parents and sisters adored Edith. It worked.

Standing together at the train station now, Edith's hand looped over Samuel's arm, they looked like they fit together. Betty was glad now that they had found each other. They made a good match.

Their wedding was a small and subdued affair in early October, much to the surprise of those who knew Edith and her propensity for grand events. They wed at a small church in North Bend, limiting guests to family and close friends. The ceremony was simple though lovely. Edith was beautiful in a white dress and veil of pale cream embroidered with white and blue flowers which her mother, Ruth, had stitched by hand. Samuel had looked the part of the handsome groom splendidly, dressed in a three-piece black suit with a light blue pocket kerchief to match the blue flowers on Edith's veil. It was when Samuel had looked at Edith, with a certain gleam in his eyes, that everyone knew the small wedding had been Edith's idea and that Samuel loved her even more because of it. The luncheon following the ceremony was equally lovely. It was held in the mess hall at the lumbermill, which seemed particularly fitting, as that is where Samuel and Edith had first laid eyes on each other.

"We're more than happy to drive," Edith then remarked, and smiled as she looked about to survey the crowd. "It's nice to be out, and we'll get to greet your Mr. Erwinshire."

Betty smiled in response. Thomas was certainly not "hers", though she let Edith's choice of words slide. Edith had been quick to refer to the orange cat, Leopold, as "your Leopold" when speaking to Betty, and just as quickly began saying "your Mr. Erwinshire." It was just her way.

Edith and Samuel, of course, had met Thomas at their wedding luncheon. The two men got along very well. In response to a question, Thomas had described the subject of the book by T.Y.L that he was publishing and distributing at

The Sapphire Key.[1] Sometime after that, he and Samuel launched into a discussion about baseball. Samuel, in fact, played baseball on the local team and invited Thomas to join the next game. From that point on, the two became friends.

"Look, the train is pulling in just now," Elizabeth declared as a passenger line rolled into the station with a soft whistle and creak of wheels, the smoke from the engine billowing into the air. In a few moments, the train came to a full stop, and the railway workers and attendees stood ready to handle the outpour of passengers soon to depart.

The four of them made their way through the pockets of people to wait. In a short while, they were obliged as the compartment doors opened and passengers began stepping out with luggage in hand. Betty glanced around to look for Thomas, but did not see him. It was hard to know which compartment of the train he would be exiting from. After a few minutes of scanning without success, a voice sounded from just behind.

"I see that I have a welcome party!"

They turned around to see Thomas striding towards them, a traveling bag in each hand. Betty smiled as his eyes met hers, feeling very glad that he had arrived back to Coos County safely.

"Thomas," Samuel greeted, and hurried over to take one of his bags. "Here, let me have that."

"Thanks," Thomas replied, handing over the bag and brushing imagined dust from the front of his vest.

"A welcome party is nothing short of necessary," Edith remarked, and smiled in greeting. "Smooth journey, I trust,

---

[1] The novel referred to here is *On the Level* by the author T.Y.L., which is about baseball. Note, T.Y.L. and his book are purely fictitious. Any reference to events or people that are based in reality, in contrast, will be noted in subsequent footnotes.

Mr. Erwinshire."

Thomas shook her offered hand. "Yes, thank you, Mrs. Clarkson." He then turned to Betty as he said, "I'm pleased to be back."

After winding through the remaining crowd and exiting the station, they finally made it to the car, a 4-door Model-T. Samuel swiftly deposited Thomas' bags inside, and took up the front driver's side alongside Edith, while Thomas, Betty, and Elizabeth filled the back.

While Edith began narrating the best way out of the station and back towards town, to Samuel's patient ear, Betty turned to Thomas.

"I'm pleased you're back too," she said. "And just in time for the book debut this week," she continued, referring to the T.Y.L book release at The Sapphire Key.

"Yes," Thomas nodded. "And the good news is, it looks like I'll be staying for it."

Betty's eyes brightened at this. It must mean that Thomas' conversations with his associate had gone well. "I'll explain more once we're back at the shop," he replied in response to her, and Elizabeth's, expectant gazes.

Betty nodded, then Elizabeth murmured, "Leopold will be pleased to see you too."

"He's waiting at the door now, I'm sure," Thomas replied with a soft laugh. The cat was not predictable in his behavior, per se, but did have certain routines that both Betty and Thomas had caught on to. Guarding the door of The Sapphire Key while they were away was one of them.

Feeling glad that they were all together, driving back into town, and eager to hear the rest of Thomas' news, Betty was content for the remainder of the ride. Before too long, they were in Marshfield, and the car rolled to a stop in front of the bookshop.

"This is where I leave you, Ms. Featherwin and Ms. Satton?" Samuel asked. "And Thomas?"

"Yes," Betty replied, and then glanced at Thomas as she continued, "And you'll be wanting to go straight to the inn." Thomas nodded in agreement with this. "Samuel, will you…"

"Yes, of course," Samuel answered. "You staying at the inn just down the road again?" He directed this question to Thomas.

"Yes, and thanks again for the ride," Thomas answered.

"You know," Edith interrupted, "There's a nice hotel in North Bend with much better accommodations."

"Oh, let him be, Edith," Samuel responded. Edith just frowned but said nothing more about it. The topic of Thomas' accommodations had come up several times before. The inn was tidy and suitable for a shorter stay, but not really the place for a longer retreat in Coos County. Time and time again, Thomas had insisted that the inn was perfectly fine and that he preferred its simplicity and convenient location. Betty did not bother him about it, but secretly thought of alternatives in the event that he made his residence in town a bit more permanent.

"All right, then," Betty said as she stepped out of the car, shaking Samuel's hand and embracing Edith.

As she turned to Thomas, he said, "How about I stop in later?"

Betty smiled, and nodded. "Yes, please do."

After another round of "goodbyes" and "see you soons," the car started up the road, and Betty and Elizabeth watched as it disappeared around the curve in the direction of the inn.

Betty took out her shop keys, and as she did so, she was not surprised to see Leopold's furry orange face pressed close to the glass pane on the door. She smiled as she entered, and was greeted by Leopold's friendly meow and inquisitive green eyes.

"He's back," she said, and received a loud purr from Leopold. She was looking forward to hearing Thomas' updates later. As Elizabeth replaced the record in the phonograph, and readied the shop for the afternoon, there was a buzz in the air that felt like hope and excitement. It also may have had a little to do with the brisk November weather.

Chapter 2

Books

After a moderately busy afternoon, Elizabeth left for the café down the street to pick up some sandwiches. There was still work to be done, and Betty and Elizabeth had decided it would be better to stay through dinner to finish up rather than leave it for the morning. In addition, they expected Thomas to come by, and were both eager to hear his news from Washington. They could all enjoy the sandwiches while catching up.

While Elizabeth was gone, Betty and Leopold remained inside of the shop. Betty sat at one of the round reading tables; Leopold sat in a chair right across from her. As she looked at the details on the sapphire lamp that adorned the tabletop, noticing the change in the lampshade's color as day faded into night, a myriad of thoughts filled her mind. Foremost was the debut of the book *On the Level* by Theodore Yousef Lamore (otherwise known as T.Y.L.). The publication process and related details had wrapped up within a couple of months, as Thomas had predicted. The book printing and shipment had been on schedule too, with Elizabeth handling the order. Now, a box of freshly printed books lay in the storage room. Betty loved the scent of new books—the ink and parchment scent—and could scarcely wait to place the books on the shelves and arrange them artfully in the shop window. The debut was in two days' time, so Thomas' arrival in Coos County could not have been better planned. He had mentioned, before he left for Washington, that he would have a short summary of the book written up that Betty could distribute to her customers.

It was a fine idea. Any new addition to the shop needed a bit of fanfare to stir customers' interest. With a new publication, promotion was especially important. Betty thought that the write-up would do just the trick, paired with the display in the shop window.

She had a feeling that there already was quite a bit of interest in the book. All news in Coos County traveled fast. It had not taken long, therefore, for the locals to learn about Thomas Erwinshire's reason for being in town. And, once Samuel Clarkson had found out about the book and its subject, the rest of the lumber boys knew about it in record time. Of course, the baseball game that Thomas had attended at Samuel's invitation in September had helped move the news along quite a bit. Although the men working at the mill were not readers for the most part, they enjoyed playing on the local baseball team, and so the subject of the book was of interest to them. Who knew that a new book at The Sapphire Key would turn a group of lumbermill workers into readers?

Betty smiled at the thought, already anticipating the swirl of activity that would occur in a couple of days. The bell on the front door jangled then, and Betty looked up to see Elizabeth at the door with a satchel in hand. Just behind her, holding another satchel, was Thomas.

"Oh, you're both here," Betty exclaimed happily. Before she could rise from her chair, Leopold leapt down with a vocal meow and began winding around Elizabeth's and Thomas' feet. He seemed torn between investigating what was inside of the satchels and greeting Thomas, alternatively sniffing and then meowing.

Elizabeth laughed, and looked down to address the cat. "Yes, I got one for you too. Just hold on a minute, will you?"

"Hello Leopold," Thomas said softly in response to the cat's repeated meows. Being addressed by both Elizabeth *and*

Thomas seemed to assuage the cat, and he finally stopped pacing and sat at Elizabeth's feet, licking his lips.

As Thomas was, for the moment, no longer of interest to Leopold, he took a sandwich out of the satchel he was holding and approached Betty. "And hello Betty," he murmured, handing the sandwich to her.

She smiled, taking it. "Thank you." She noticed, as she met his eyes, how the tint of hazel in them changed as day faded into night. Just like the sapphire lamps. It was odd and beautiful.

"I ran into Elizabeth just as she was coming up the road with these," Thomas explained.

"Good timing," Betty responded, and gestured for Thomas to place his coat on the coatrack. As he did so, she took the rest of the sandwiches out and arranged them neatly on the front counter, along with napkins. They smelled delicious. It was no wonder that Leopold had been so eager. He was already situated on the entryway rug, digging into a tuna sandwich that Elizabeth had bought for him. He was, fortunately, a tidy and meticulous eater, and so Betty had no qualms about allowing him to eat in the shop. Every time he ate with her and her mother at home, he kept his meal confined to his area, and always cleaned his plate and washed his face. For a cat, he was startingly well-mannered during mealtimes—just a bit overeager *before* eating.

"Here you are," Betty said as Thomas returned. He took a seat before her at the counter, where Betty had placed a roasted vegetable sandwich.

"Excellent," Thomas responded. "Thanks for this."

Elizabeth, who had just taken a bite, merely shook her head and waved a hand. Thomas understood her meaning.

Betty jumped in. "Please, tell us your news. And how was the train? I hope the journey wasn't too tiring."

"No, not too bad at all. Even with the rain, we weren't slowed up that much." He paused to take a bite of the sandwich. "And I've unpacked. Everything is spic and span at the inn. Oh, and I have the book summary for you. I'll bring it by tomorrow."

Betty nodded. She appreciated these updates, though was eager to get to the real news. Thomas anticipated this, for he continued, "Now, to the important news."

"You mentioned that you'd be staying for the book debut?" Elizabeth inquired.

"Yes, how did you manage that?" Betty could not resist asking.

Thomas gave a short laugh. "You seem skeptical. But, in truth, the job of convincing John was not as difficult as we thought it might be. It turns out that this book deal is priority for us right now. Once I suggested that it would be better if I stayed in Marshfield to oversee the distribution here, John actually agreed with me."

"Doesn't that mean he'll have to stay put to manage the office?"

"That's the other piece of it. While I've been away, one of our editors resigned. Instead of looking to fill the space with another editor—goodness knows we don't need one—John has been looking for another associate."

Betty's eyes widened. "Are you okay with that?"

Thomas daubed his chin with a napkin, and answered, "I am, actually. I'd received a telegram from John telling me about this plan, but it had slipped my mind. We talked it over, and it does make sense. With another associate, there'll be someone to manage the office. That will allow John to resume traveling. It would be an overall benefit." He described their arrangements to debut T.Y.L.'s book in various other locations—including bookstores in Pasco, Washington and

San Francisco, California, and later on, in New York and Massachusetts—that John would be heading up over the next couple of months, necessitating travel. The sooner that they could find and hire an in-office associate, therefore, the better. With Coos County being the first debut location, it was important that someone from the office oversee it. Thomas, of course, had been the obvious choice. John would oversee the other locations.

Betty and Elizabeth nodded in agreement.

"That seems to have settled things for the time being," Betty remarked.

"It has, rather," Thomas responded. "And I am glad. I wanted to be here for the book debut."

Betty could see in his eyes that he wanted to be here for other reasons as well, but he did not wish to voice those in front of Elizabeth. It was their secret, Thomas' and Betty's: the secret of Thomas' parentage. For Betty, it was her third secret, the first being her unfortunate first name and the second being her ability to understand and communicate with Leopold. This third secret continued to tug at her. Betty presumed that it would continue to do so until she and Thomas had a chance to speak about it. She was eager to pick up on where they had left off before he traveled to Washington. Now, however, was neither the time nor place for it.

"Well, I'm glad too," Elizabeth responded, not cognizant of the silent exchange between Thomas and Betty. "It will be good to have you here early on Thursday to help with the book display and the handouts."

"Be careful, she's ready to put you to work," Betty teased, to which Elizabeth creased her forehead in mock indignation.

Thomas laughed. "I'm happy to help. Speaking of which, how is the condition of the books? I sent my specifications directly to printing…"

Thus, after finishing their sandwiches, the three of them (plus Leopold) spent the remainder of the hour planning for Thursday. Betty showed Thomas the box of books in the storage room, and, after inspecting them with the eye of a scrupulous editor, Thomas was satisfied. They then returned to the front of the shop and prepared to lock up for the evening. They engaged in casual conversation until they reached the Featherwin house, which was their point of parting. Elizabeth waved them goodbye to go the short distance further to her own house. Instead of leaving in turn, Thomas remained with Betty for a moment.

The evening was calm and quiet. Not even a seagull or a foghorn in the distance interrupted them. Betty was the first to break the silence.

"I've been thinking a lot about the photograph."

Thomas nodded. "Me too."

"Have you had any insights?" Betty asked hopefully, though Thomas merely sighed and shook his head. After their moment of revelation about the photograph that Betty had been given by Mrs. Highley, they were filled with hope. This was a photo of Mrs. Highley's sister, Sarah, standing next to Thomas' mother. They were optimistic that this would be one step closer to seeking the answers Thomas craved. He felt that speaking to Mrs. Highley would clear things up for him. And so, Betty had arranged for them to have tea with her the following week.

Mrs. Highley was pleasant and welcoming, as usual, and had made a place for them to enjoy tea and pastries on the back porch, which faced the sea. After exchanging pleasantries, Betty took out the photograph, which she had promised to return to her. Mrs. Highley then asked them if they had found the photograph useful.

She did not know Thomas very well before the tea, but this changed dramatically afterwards. Thomas told her about his upbringing and his desire to learn more about his mother. He explained why the photograph meant so much to him. After hearing all of this, Mrs. Highley flat-out insisted that Thomas keep the photograph. It was the least she could do, she said, because she could not give them any further information. Despite their questions about the possible connection between May Bell Sebastian and Sarah Mitchell, Mrs. Highley was at a loss. She could only assume (as Thomas and Betty had already assumed) that her sister had been friends with May Bell in 1890. Beyond that, the rest was a mystery.

The remainder of their time at the Highley residence was spent pleasantly enough. Betty and Thomas enjoyed their refreshments, and Mrs. Highley seemed to enjoy getting to know Thomas. When they departed, they thanked Mrs. Highley, and were grateful for her openness and generosity. Still, they could not help but feel disappointed. The answers to their questions felt so out of reach.

This seemed to bother Thomas much more than he let on. Over the past couple of months, Betty caught him taking the photograph out of his pocket and looking at it intensely, as if doing so would bring him clarity. Every time Thomas realized that Betty had caught him, he swiftly replaced the photograph in his pocket and said nothing about it. Betty knew better than to pester him, but that did not prevent her from thinking about it herself.

"We'll find more information, I just know it," Betty murmured to reassure him. He smiled at her efforts, though she could tell he was not convinced.

"Well, I'll let you go in," Thomas responded at length, and bent down to pat Leopold.

"All right," Betty replied. As he stood back up, she added, "I'm glad you're back."

He smiled then. "I wasn't gone for very long."

"Regardless," Betty responded, shaking her head. "I'm glad."

"Well, good. I am too," Thomas conceded, and Leopold meowed as though in agreement. "Lunch tomorrow?" he then asked, referring to their usual routine.

"Of course," Betty smiled, and with that, Thomas took her hand and dipped his head good night. He made sure she and Leopold entered the house all right before giving a final wave and turning down the road.

Chapter 3

Sales & Lampshades

In late autumn and winter in Coos County, time passed by quickly. The days were shorter, colder, and busier, with folks rising early to attend to business and turning in early too. When night fell with a cold rush of damp air, a whispering wind came along with it, encouraging those still out and about to take shelter indoors. This month of November was particularly intemperate in its abundance of rain and drop in temperature that foretold of the snow that would arrive in December.

Thus, the morning of the book debut arrived cold and rainy, and Betty rose early to run through the day's events in her head. She hoped the weather would not deter customers. By the number of people who had passed by the shop display window the evening prior, however, there was a good chance that The Sapphire Key would receive visitors regardless of the rain. She and Elizabeth had arranged the window before closing up the shop for the evening. They propped several of the books on stands, and placed others across a blue tablecloth that complemented the blue lettering of the book's title. To decorate and enhance the display, Betty also placed several baseballs and a mitt in the window. She had found these items tucked away in a corner of the storage room, as chance would have it. They must have belonged to her father, from long ago, although she could not recall a time when he had played. She wondered what other hidden treasures she might find, and made a mental note to explore the crevices of the storage room later.

As Betty slipped on her rainboots, preparing to step out

and grab a quick bite in the kitchen on her way, Bea Featherwin, Betty's loving and concerned mother, halted her in her tracks. While Betty was an adult, she was also a daughter and Bea's motherly instinct still played a role in her life. Betty had inherited some of her father's stubbornness, so Bea could not stop Betty from doing what she set her mind to. She could, however, offer advice and alternatives. In this spirit, she urged Betty to call on Clarence or Samuel at the mill and ask for a ride to the shop in the car.

"Wouldn't it be better to get a ride in this weather? You're out in the rain so often these days," Bea commented, standing in the kitchen with a hand on her hip as she watched Betty putting on her gloves in the parlor. Bea was still dressed in a flour-covered apron. She had been baking this morning, and the scent of buttermilk biscuits wafted in the air. The tea kettle steamed on the stove. Betty had set her half-full cup of jasmine tea on the kitchen table, unfinished.

Betty merely sighed with a soft shake of her head. She did not like to impose, especially as she had been given a ride from Samuel just recently. It was too early to send a note, and too cumbersome to make a telephone call, in any case.

"Mother, you know the book debut is today and I need to be there soon. It's really not raining hard at all," she protested. This was true, for the rain certainly was not as bad as it *could* be. She was ready to disagree with Bea further, though was saved the trouble. A knock sounded at the door which interrupted their dialogue. Bea opened it to see Thomas at the threshold with a large, black umbrella in one hand, a spare umbrella in the other, and a jacket folded over his arm.

"Good morning, Mrs. Featherwin," he greeted with a smile.

Bea could not hide her contentment as she replied, "Oh,

Mr. Erwinshire, this is a nice surprise. I see you've made it back from Washington."

"Yes. I thought I would accompany your daughter to the bookshop, if that's all right. I'm on my way there now." With his smile and pleasant demeanor, coupled with the fact that he had arrived with the extra umbrella and coat, there was simply no way Bea could refuse his request. Betty knew that, and smiled as she watched the two at the door. Feeling rather pleased when she heard her mother assent, she crossed over to them as she slipped the handle of her bag over her shoulder. Thomas nodded in greeting and handed her his spare umbrella.

"Be safe, now, and best wishes for success today," Bea said. "And, Mr. Erwinshire, you must come for tea soon."

Thomas dipped his head slightly, saying, "You're very kind."

Betty smiled as they waved Bea goodbye. Thomas had received more invitations to tea than she could keep track of over the past several months.

The rain was coming down in a steady drizzle. Thomas waited as Betty opened the umbrella, and then they both started on their way down the street.

"Thank you for coming," Betty remarked. "You arrived at just the right moment."

Thomas looked over at her with an air of self-assurance. "You're welcome." He then looked down and around and asked, "Where's Leopold?" The cat, who usually accompanied Betty everywhere, was nowhere to be seen.

Betty carefully stepped over a rain puddle. "Oh, I told him to go on ahead of me. He should be at the shop by now." She spoke in an unconcerned way, and it was only after she spoke that her cheeks flushed as she realized her slip-up.

"Oh, I see. Hopefully he's found somewhere dry until we

arrive," Thomas replied nonchalantly.

Betty let out a breath. Clearly, Thomas did not consider what she had just said to be odd. He had seen her talk to Leopold before, and even *he* talked to the cat sometimes. However, it was always lighthearted and not with the intent that Leopold could understand and communicate back. Lately, though, Betty sensed that she really could talk to Leopold and that he could respond. Just last week while she and her mother were chatting in the parlor after dinner, Leopold meowed in such a way that surprised Betty. It was not a normal meow. It was as though he were enunciating. If the notion was not so bizarre, she would have sworn that she heard him say, "yes, I think so." Bea did not seem to notice, as she continued on with their conversation without pause. This made Betty wonder if perhaps only *she* could understand the cat. If so, then perhaps this secret could remain safe. Still, she cautioned herself to be more careful.

"Betty?" Thomas' voice interrupted her thoughts. "I asked if there is anything else you need for the book display."

"Oh, I'm sorry," she replied, looking over at him. She had not heard him speak, consumed as she was in her own thoughts about Leopold. "No, nothing else. Actually, I think you'll rather like the display," she continued, recovering herself. She smiled and a sparkle shone in her eyes as she added, "I found something perfect to add to it last night after you left." She referred to the baseballs and mitt she had found in the storage room.

"Is that so? More perfect than my write-up?"

They shared a laugh as they approached the bookshop, with the words 'The Sapphire Key' emblazoned in gold-leaf on the door. Closing their umbrellas, they nestled underneath the small awning as Betty took out her key to unlock the door. Just as she did so, they heard a meow, and

Leopold came forward to greet them. His fur was slightly damp, though it appeared as though he had found a snug area for shelter.

"There we are," she announced to admit them inside, and Leopold at once headed for his cushion underneath the phonograph to curl up. Betty proceeded to lay her belongings down and part the curtains throughout.

"Well, I have to say, job well-done." Thomas' voice sounded from the front of the shop.

Betty turned around from where she stood, at the window by the far bookcase, and saw Thomas looking at the book display. She smiled, and responded, "So you like it, then."

Thomas drew himself away and parted the last set of curtains for her. "Did you borrow the baseballs from Samuel?"

"Actually, no. I found them in the storage room."

"Oh, really?" Thomas responded, raising his brows. "Did your father used to play?" He knew that her father, Henry Featherwin, established The Sapphire Key, and had managed it successfully before his passing two years ago. He had entrusted Betty with it, and had left behind all manner of odds and ends in the storage room. The coatrack was there, as well as pieces of old furniture; old notebooks and shop ledgers; and a great many other items that Betty had not had the time to investigate.

Betty shrugged and said, "He must have." She smiled then, and murmured, "There are a lot of things I found out about him later on from my mother. I'll have to ask her about baseball as well."

"You are fortunate that you can ask her, and that you have these memories of him," Thomas replied with a tone of sincerity mixed with sadness that made Betty suddenly want to reach out and comfort him. She knew that the photograph of his mother, May, and the mystery attached to it, still bothered him. She also knew that, despite his outward show of resilience, he had a space in his heart that longed to be filled with memories of his mother that he simply did not have.

She placed a hand on his arm softly, though could say no words then, as the bell on the door jangled to announce the arrival of Elizabeth. A glance passed between her and Thomas, with the promise that they would revisit their contemplations on the photograph later.

◌৪

The morning passed by in a blink, and the shop was soon filled with customers admiring the book display, taking copies of the handout that Thomas had prepared, and lining up at the counter to make their purchases. The weather did not impede customers from visiting the shop; on the contrary, it encouraged them. The Sapphire Key was a welcome shelter out of the rain. Its cozy and inviting environment drew readers in, and Betty had spent time sprucing up the Reading Room for those who desired to stay awhile and begin reading. This room, which was towards the back of the stop, was specifically designed by Betty as a space for relaxing and reading. It had a fireplace, sumptuous couches, and coffee tables. This is also where she kept her antiques and collectibles, secured in a glass cabinet for all to admire. She was pleased to see folks milling in and out of the Reading Room after they made their purchase of *On the Level*, and equally pleased that the hype about the book had proved fruitful.

In short, the debut was a success. At the end of the afternoon, as Elizabeth was tallying the number of sales, she called Betty over to the counter. She had her glasses perched atop her head and she was studying her ledger with an expression of disbelief on her face.

"What is it?" Betty asked, with a tone of slight concern.

"Well, just that we'll have to order in a second shipment of books. They've sold like hotcakes today!"

Betty smiled broadly. "That's wonderful."

"And," Elizabeth continued, and shuffled through the papers on the counter until she found the one that she was looking for. "You won't believe the order request we received. Look here." She showed a request slip to Betty. Although order requests were rare, customers did, on occasion, send in a request for a book or magazine. Oftentimes, the request was for something that Betty did not ordinarily keep in stock, such as an archived periodical or an edition that was out-of-print. As she looked at the slip, however, she saw that it was *not* the usual request. On the request slip was printed, "L.J. Simpson. Requesting ten (10) copies of book 'On the Level' by author T.Y.L."

Betty looked at Elizabeth, the surprise in her eyes surely

mirroring the sentiment she saw on Elizabeth's face. L.J. Simpson, the founder and former mayor of North Bend, lived high on the cliffs in a mansion overlooking the pier and harbor of the Coos Bay region. He lived in splendor, as the rumor went, and often traveled when he was not hosting a party on his estate. He rarely, if ever, ventured below the cliffs into town. It was a wonder, therefore, to hold a request with his name on it in her hand. It was an honor too, and Betty would be sure to get the shipment to him as soon as possible. It made her wonder whether he enjoyed reading, or baseball, or both.[2]

❧

The end of the day brought relief. Although it had been a rewarding day, it had also been tiring. Thomas had left after the initial morning rush, though Betty and Elizabeth had worked the whole day and straight through lunch. Betty was quite ready to lock up for the evening and head home with Leopold. She was sure she would fall asleep the second her face touched her pillow. Leopold, who had an eventful day himself with a great deal of attention from all of the customers, was already snoozing on his cushion.

Betty had sent Elizabeth home as the clock struck a quarter past five, and now only she and Leopold remained. She glanced around the shop fondly, feeling that her father must be proud. She had kept the shop alive, and therein kept her father's spirit alive. There was work to be done yet, but for now, the fruit of a long day's work was enough of an accomplishment. All was well.

The last thing she needed to do was go to the storage room. She smiled as she passed the sleeping Leopold on her way there to gather her coat. As she went inside, her eyes traveled to the spot where she had found the baseballs and mitt. How peculiar to find just the items that would complete

---

[2] Louis Jerome Simpson was indeed the real-life founder and mayor of North Bend, Oregon, and lived on a sprawling estate called Shore Acres on the cliffs of Coos Bay. It is uncertain whether he was an avid reader. He did, however, build a baseball park and sponsor a baseball team in North Bend.

her book display, she thought.

She folded her coat over her arm and turned to leave, but paused. A feeling of curiosity took hold of her suddenly, and she retreated towards the back of the storage room. Her hand brushed the shelf that had housed the mitt, and that also contained an old stack of newspapers. She would need to go through those someday. As she continued to look around, a piece of furniture that she had not seen before caught her eye. It was not a small piece of furniture; on the contrary, it was a large desk. She was surprised that it had escaped her notice. In all her visits to this room, she could not recall seeing it before. On coming closer, it looked to be a writing desk. The craftmanship was impressive, and the material was a deep mahogany. The feet were carved with an intricate design and, as she peered closer, she noticed a hint of gold embedded into the mahogany. She also noticed that the desk had a long drawer with a gold handle and a key hole. She was sure that she would be unable to open the drawer, as it would likely be locked and she had no idea where to begin looking for a key. Still, she tried the drawer.

To her astonishment, it opened. More astonishing still was that there was something inside of the drawer. Feeling inside, she found a slip of paper. Carefully taking it out, she unfolded it. It was faded, but the ink was still visible. It appeared to be a receipt of some kind, likely for printing or shipping. These receipts were common, and were heavily used. Upon further inspection, however, Betty's assumption was proven incorrect.

The receipt was for four Tiffany lamps, blue/lavender baroque. The price listed was six hundred dollars.

Betty gasped and nearly dropped the receipt. She suddenly realized a number of things in rapid succession. The sapphire lamps in the bookshop, which were the shop's namesake, were Tiffany lamps. Henry Featherwin had not been given the sapphire lamps by a foreign trader (as he had claimed), but had spent his own money on them. He had never told Betty, or Bea, about this purchase.

Now, this mahogany writing desk resided in the shop along with a receipt which revealed something she had not known about her father before. She felt odd in this revelation, similar to what Thomas may have felt upon seeing a photograph of his mother for the first time.

As she stepped out of the storage room and headed towards the front door, beckoning Leopold to her, she felt that perhaps she would not fall asleep so quickly tonight.

Chapter 4

Woodwork

"Where would you like me to put this?" Elizabeth Satton asked.

Betty and Elizabeth were in The Sapphire Key the day after the book debut. As the debut had gone so well, only twenty copies of the book remained in stock. Elizabeth had already prepared a request for another shipment. She now stood at the counter, holding in her hand a printed notice that stated,

> *Thank You Coos Bay for a successful debut of 'On the Level', a novel by T.Y.L. The Sapphire Key appreciates your business and support! We will have more books in stock soon. In the meantime, please explore our other selections.*

Betty walked over to her to take a look at the notice, nodding in approval. "I think the window display is the best place," she responded, indicating the shopfront book display where two of the remaining books lay propped on bookstands. Elizabeth took one of the books off of a stand, setting it next to the other book, and arranged the notice on the stand instead. She stepped back to assess her handiwork, received another approving nod from Betty, and then returned to the counter to finish up the book order request.

Betty surveyed the shop in appreciation. She was pleased that book sales had far exceeded her, and Thomas', expectations. She had not spoken to him since yesterday, and she looked forward to telling him the good news.

As her eyes scanned the shop, they came to rest on the

sapphire lamps adorning the reading tables. The blue lampshades seemed to glimmer with kaleidoscopic hues in the morning light. Betty had a new regard for the lamps now after her discovery in the storage room, and had awoken this morning with a new perspective. After arriving home at a reasonable hour last night, eating dinner with Bea, and turning in early, she rose feeling remarkably refreshed. She had thought about her startling find before falling asleep with Leopold curled up beside her. It had been a surprise to find the antique mahogany writing desk, and the receipt for the lamps, but not particularly unusual. She anticipated coming across odds and ends in the storage room. In Henry's time, the room was used to store just about everything, from surplus books to hatboxes. Thus, it did not strike her as odd to find the mitt and baseballs on a neglected top shelf. Likewise, it was not so odd for the writing desk to be there. The fact is, while Henry had always planned to clean out and organize the storage room and had made plans to auction off or sell the old furniture, he never got to it. Worse yet, Betty never got to it.

There were reasons for that. The flu had crept up on Henry in a quick and brutal way, leaving little time to make preparations for things like cleaning or organizing. Shop maintenance was a small and unimportant task at the time, as compared to other things. When Betty had assumed ownership of The Sapphire Key and began the remodel, she did not think to touch the storage room. In one sense, it seemed too large of an undertaking to contemplate. In another sense, Betty had felt it disrespectful to disturb the room that held so many of Henry's belongings. So, the remodel was completed, and the years continued on, and still the storage room remained in its original state. As if Henry had never left.

Even now, Betty considered the items in the storage room to be Henry's. Regardless of what he had said to her, or what the paperwork for the shop said, those items were his. The old stack of newspapers sat upon the shelf, still ready for Henry to come by and take a page to read as he ate his lunch. The footstool against the wall (which he had used countless times to reach a book on a high shelf, or as a way to prop open the door) was undisturbed in its spot, ready to be used again. Sometimes, when Betty entered to hang her coat on the coatrack, she thought she could detect the faint aroma of dark coffee that she had always associated with her father. It was only for a moment, but the scent was there.

There were, undoubtedly, many items in the storage room, accumulated over the years, that Betty had yet to discover. And so, the mitt, the baseballs, and the antique writing desk were not surprising finds. The receipt for the lamps should not be surprising either. Betty held a great deal of reverence for her father and his decisions, and supposed that there must be a good reason for him not to tell her the truth about the value of the lamps. Betty thus resolved, for the time being, to keep the discovery to herself. Henry clearly wanted it that way, and so, out of respect for him, and to preserve the story of the lamps, she would stay silent about it. Everyone believed that Henry had indeed been gifted the lamps by a foreign trader[3], and that they were beautiful, although cheap, imports of some kind. Now Betty knew that the lamps were not cheap, but rather that they were quite valuable. They were crafted from the finest stained glass, which accounted for the lampshades' vibrant, exotic colors and the sensation of changing hues between morning and

---

[3] *See* Gross, Sarah Jane. "Chapter 2: The Bookshop." *The Two Secrets.* Sarah Jane Gross, 2020.

night. Sold in specialty stores only as a luxury item, their cost ran in the hundreds of dollars.[4] It was a wonder that Henry had been able to acquire four of them ten years ago, and at the overall modest price of six hundred dollars. As Betty glanced at the lamps now, she actually preferred that everyone kept on believing in the myth of their acquisition. Who knew what could happen if word got out of their actual value?

All in all, keeping the lamps' true value secret would be best. Betty thought she would, one day soon, move the mahogany writing desk to the Reading Room, as it would match the existing furniture nicely. She would keep the receipt, however, hidden.

ॐ

During lunch, Betty had a chance to talk with Thomas about the great success of the book sales. He was very pleased, and planned to place a call to his associate, John, to share the news. Thomas also had a bit of his own news. As they sat together in the café, sipping coffee and eating sandwiches (with Leopold indulging in a plate of surfperch fish[5]), Thomas took an envelope out of his pocket and placed it in the center of the table.

"Is that your news?" Betty asked, looking down at the envelope curiously.

"One piece of it," Thomas answered with a smile. "But

---

[4] The sapphire lamps are based upon antique collector's Tiffany lamps, produced by Louis Comfort Tiffany (Tiffany Studios) from the 1890s through the 1920s. They were a valuable and expensive product found in well-to-do households.

[5] Surfperch is a fish common to Oregon. They are slim, saucer-shaped fish that can reach two pounds in weight.

before I share it, I want to say thank you."

Betty raised an eyebrow. "For what?"

"For partnering with us on the book distribution. I could not have wished for a better match."

Betty smiled and tucked a loose strand of hair behind her ear. "I should be thanking you as well, for entrusting us with that manuscript."

"There was never a question in my mind," Thomas answered.

Betty thought of everything that had occurred since she had met Thomas, and along the same line, she added, "It led to a successful book debut, but apart from that, it led me to your mother's poem." She referred to finding Thomas' bookmark inside of the manuscript, which had the lines of a poem written upon it. The poem had been by May Bell Sebastian, Betty's favorite poet and Thomas' long-deceased mother.

"Yes, it did," Thomas replied. "And it led me closer to her in the process. Speaking of which…" He set down his coffee cup and gestured towards the envelope.

Betty looked at him with a question in her eyes, and he nodded to indicate that she could open it. She reached over to take the envelope and opened the flap to see what lay inside. She then took out two photographs. Both looked well-preserved, with not a single tear or crease. Carefully, Betty laid them out in front of her. One was a photograph of a woman dressed in fashion reminiscent of the 1890s. It was styled in the manner of a portrait, with the woman standing tall and looking straight at what must have been the cameraman. The other was of a house in the foreground, and a windmill in the background. At the base of the windmill was the shadowed figure of a woman. Betty was not sure what to make of the house and the windmill, though she felt the portrait of the woman to be familiar.

She studied it for a second longer, and then asked, "Is this your mother?"

"It is."

Betty returned her gaze to Thomas, and saw that he looked pleased.

"That was a portrait taken of her, sometime in the 1890s."

Betty nodded. "Yes, that's what I would have guessed." She turned the photograph around, but to her disappointment, there was no identifying language on the back.

"No help there," Thomas said, as he watched her turn the photograph over, and continued, "I found these when I was back in Washington. These are the photos my aunt Violet gave to me a couple of years ago."

"Did she say anything about them at the time?" Betty inquired hopefully, though from what Thomas had explained to her before about Violet, she guessed that the answer would be "no." Seeing Thomas shake his head, she saw that her guess was correct.

"I only wish she did," he said. "So, they were a bit useless to me for a while."

Betty was somewhat surprised at his descriptor "useless," and before she could reply, he clarified, "I knew that the portrait was supposed to be my mother, but I had no way to verify it. And, at the time, I was not feeling very trusting of Violet."

She nodded, understanding his predicament.

"But…" he continued, "…putting this together with the photograph from Mrs. Highley gives me that confirmation. I know that this is a portrait of *her* now. And, I've been thinking that these pictures all could have been taken at around the same time."

"Oh," Betty exclaimed, and felt flooded with a sense of hope. "So, you did have some insights. That's wonderful, Thomas!"

He smiled, though waved his hand and said, "Well, let's not get ahead of ourselves quite yet. I still need your help. You *did* promise that we would be in this together," he teased.

Betty gave a soft laugh. "I did indeed, and I admit that I would be quite let down if you figured out everything on your own."

"Well, good. Because I have a proposition for you."

Betty tilted her head in thoughtful expectation.

"What do you say about writing to Mrs. Highley's sister?"

Betty was pleased at this suggestion, and in fact had been thinking on it herself. She did not wish to bring it up, on the chance that Thomas would not be ready for that step. It appeared that now he was.

"I think that's a brilliant idea," she said. "If Mrs. Highley's sister knew your mother, as we suspect, then surely she is the best person to reach out to."

Thomas nodded, and murmured, "I only hope that she'll be receptive to it."

Betty smiled then, and said, "Don't worry about that. I'll pay a visit to Mrs. Highley and ask for her sister's address. She knows how important this is to you. I'm sure she'll tell me whether it would be worth sending it."

Betty gathered up the photographs and replaced them to the envelope, then handed the envelope back to Thomas.

"Thank you," he said, holding her hand for just a moment longer before releasing it and slipping the envelope into the pocket of his jacket.

Betty took a bite of her sandwich, digesting this news, and then remembered that the envelope had only been one part of Thomas' news. "What is your other news?"

"Well," Thomas replied, after taking a final bite of his own sandwich, "This is something rather fun. Did you know that Samuel Clarkson spends the weekends in November crafting wares from the extra wood scraps at the mill? He makes wooden toys for the local children."

"No, I didn't know," Betty replied with a smile. She did not know this particular fact about Samuel, though was not all together surprised. For having a serious nature in general, Samuel was lighthearted in spirit. He enjoyed hard work as much as merrymaking, as was evidenced by his evenings at the dance hall with Edith and weekends on the baseball field. Betty was also not surprised to hear about the use of wood scraps to make goods. It brought her back to her childhood days, when she would visit the mill with her father during Christmastime and would come home with gifts of wooden figurines. She proceeded to explain this to Thomas. "I am not surprised to hear that Samuel makes toys. When I was a child, I would visit the mill with my father at around this time. Many of the mill workers were very skilled at carving and would make gifts out of spare myrtle wood."

Thomas nodded. "He told me that he starts in November so that the gifts will be ready for Christmas next month." Thomas further explained that Samuel ordinarily had the general store in town sell them. Ruth Smithson, Samuel's mother-in-law, also sold them in her giftshop in North Bend. "It's been a sort of hobby for him, and he creates all of the toys down at the lumberyard during his time off."

Betty smiled. Samuel reminded her a bit of the men that her father had worked with, years ago, who were kindhearted and spent their leisure time making good use of the spare wood to bring a smile to a child's face. Samuel's likeness to these men was heartening. "It is generous of him," she responded. "And you sound interested."

"I am interested," Thomas replied. "Actually, Samuel has invited me to assist him in making small wooden cars and boats for the children."

"Oh, how nice!" Betty remarked, and was again made to reminisce of the pleasant times she had spent with her father, watching the men craft wooden gifts. It felt somewhat full-circle to hear of Samuel doing the same thing now. "Will you go and help him?"

"Well, that's my news," Thomas answered with a smile, seeming pleased at Betty's positive reaction to the idea. "I do plan to go. I think I'll enjoy it, as I rarely have the opportunity to do something like this back in Washington. Plus, it will take my mind off of things."

Betty took his final remark to refer to Thomas' enduring thoughts about his mother. It would certainly be good for him to clear his mind of those thoughts, if only for a while. And she, too, thought that he would enjoy it. If nothing else, it would be something different to do, and would bolster his friendship with Samuel.

"I agree," she commented. "When are you going?"

"It'll be this Saturday. I'll meet Samuel at the mill in the morning and stay through the afternoon, so you likely won't see me."

"Oh," Betty replied, thinking it was considerate of him to let her know of his plans. "Well, I'm very glad that you're going. It will do the both of you some good. I look forward to seeing what you create."

"So do I," Thomas replied with a smile. "I haven't done woodwork in a while, so this will be a bit of an experiment. It'll be good to try my hand at it again."

Betty nodded in agreement, pleased that he had this occasion to look forward to. She decided to tell him about the wooden carvings she still had from her childhood. There were five, small, myrtle wood animal carvings (sea creatures, plus a cat), lined up on the mantelpiece at home. She recalled that her father's favorite was the cat figurine. It was a rather ordinary carving, as compared to the more intricate carvings of turtles and seals. Even so, each carving was unique, from the shade of the wood to the grooves that were made to create the eyes and mouth, and the smooth texture.

"I'm glad," Thomas responded, after she told him that she was thus excited to see the result of Samuel's and Thomas' work. "And I'll put forth my best effort," he assured, hinting that his woodworking skills were modest. There was a twinkle in his hazel eyes as he said the words, though, that made Betty believe that he was far more talented than he was letting on.

She smiled in return, and said, "I'd expect nothing less." As she paused to take a sip of her drink, another idea came to her. "You know, if you have no plans for Saturday evening, why don't we have a dinner party after you and Samuel finish up at the mill?"

Thomas appeared in favor of this suggestion. "Well, that sounds great."

"Mother has been asking you over to tea, but this will be much better. Samuel and Edith can join us too."

"Fine idea," Thomas responded. "But, are you sure your mother won't mind?"

"No, she won't mind," Betty replied, already seeing Bea light up at the prospect of hosting a party where she would have the chance to cook and get to know Thomas. It was a perfect resolution to Bea's and Edith's recent requests that Thomas join them for tea.

Thus, in the span of the lunch hour, several things were decided. Thomas and Betty would prepare a letter to send to Mrs. Highley's sister, Sarah. Thomas and Samuel would work on wooden carvings at the mill. And, the Featherwins would host a dinner party.

There was much to do, though more importantly, much to look forward to.

Chapter 5

Who's Sleeping?

Betty awoke with a start to a loud noise. She quickly sat up in bed, her heart hammering, and looked around the room. Leopold had jumped onto the dresser and knocked books to the floor, along with the other items that had been arranged there. He stretched out across the top of the dresser and looked down at her, his big green eyes twinkling in the darkness, and his large back and front paws hanging slightly over the edge. He had no idea how big he was.

"Well, Mr. Leopold," Betty muttered groggily, "What was the reason for that?" She looked at the clock and saw that it was five-o-clock in the morning. It was far too early to be awake, and yet, as she moved to pull back her covers, she heard a noise down the hall towards the kitchen. Perplexed, she stood and fastened her robe around her, then opened the door and quietly walked in the direction of the kitchen. With a soft thumping sound, Leopold leapt down from the dresser and padded along after her.

As they approached, Betty could detect a blissful aroma. Her mother, Bea, had placed some of her homemade biscuits in the oven to bake. She was standing near the oven, wearing her oven mitts and an apron. It appeared that she had been awake for a little while.

"Mother," Betty greeted, "What are you doing up at this hour?"

Bea turned to Betty with a soft smile, removing her oven mitts and setting them on the kitchen table. "Well, dear, I just couldn't sleep, so I thought I might as well get up and start cooking." She then took a seat across from her and continued, "I was careful to be quiet, as I didn't want to wake you and Leopold."

"Oh, we were already awake," Betty replied with a sigh, and pulled the sleeves of her robe down to warm her arms against the slight chill in the air. "It's not your fault—Leopold made quite a bit of noise on his own." She turned an accusatory gaze towards the cat, who was now sitting in the doorway to the kitchen, cleaning his face with a paw.

"Oh, I'm sorry," Bea responded with a subtle laugh in her voice. "Do you want to rest up a little longer before you leave for The Sapphire Key?"

Betty turned her gaze back to Bea, and shook her head. "No, thanks. I couldn't fall back asleep now. What are you cooking? I'll help."

"Well, I'm just about to put on some tea," Bea replied, indicating the tea kettle that sat upon the stove. "If you do that, then I'll whip up some eggs with the biscuits."

Betty nodded in agreement with this plan and set about boiling the water for the tea, while Bea fetched eggs from the icebox. In a short while, they both sat with steaming cups of lemon tea with a dash of ginger, and a plateful of scrambled eggs and biscuits along with Bea's homemade raspberry jam. Betty was not sure whether it was the enticing smell of the food, or the fact that she had worked up an appetite with the long hours she had spent working of late, but the meal was delicious. She could not recall when she had enjoyed a meal this much, though also could not recall waking early enough to assist her mother with breakfast. It was quite nice to spend the early morning hour with Bea, and now she was almost thankful that Leopold had awoken her. He seemed to enjoy this morning time as well, for he sat tucked comfortably in the doorway watching them with a soft purr in his throat.

It was just five-thirty once they finished, which was still

early yet, and gave Betty plenty of time to freshen up and dress. Before six, Betty was at the front door, fully dressed in boots and raincoat. She told Bea that she planned to leave for the shop early to get a head start on work that had been left behind from the previous day. It would be quiet, undisturbed time for her to accomplish a lot, she reasoned. Before heading out, she wrapped two biscuits with a bit of jam into a napkin and tucked them inside of her shoulder bag. She intended to enjoy them later.

Betty waved her mother goodbye, and then she and Leopold stepped out of the door to begin their walk to the bookshop. It was a cool, dank morning, though no rain yet. Betty started on her way, thinking about which tasks she would tackle first when she arrived, when she heard a voice behind her. She paused and turned, as she recognized the voice as belonging to Thomas. *Could it be that he's up early too?'* she wondered in disbelief. The answer turned out to be, *yes, indeed.* Thomas approached with a swift step to catch up with her and Leopold. He likewise looked as if he had already been awake for some time. He was dressed in shirtsleeves and a deep gray vest and matching gray slacks. He also wore a cap, and his jacket was folded over his arm.

Betty smiled in greeting, and asked, "Thomas, why are you up so early?"

Thomas smiled back at her with the rejoinder, "I could ask you the same thing. Did Leopold wake you?" His tone was teasing, and he did not expect her to reply in the affirmative.

"As a matter of fact, he did. I hope a cat didn't wake you up as well," she responded with a soft laugh.

"No," he smiled back. "I just couldn't sleep, so decided to get ready and go on down to the café for breakfast." He looked over at her and his eyes brightened as he asked,

"Would you like to join me?"

"Oh, that sounds lovely," Betty replied. "I've already had breakfast, but I would enjoy a cup of coffee."

Pleased with this plan, Betty and Leopold changed their course to accompany Thomas to their usual café by the pier. At this early hour, there was just one other person inside of the café—a man—sitting at a table with a newspaper in his hands. The paper obscured his face, though it appeared as though he were reading its contents intently.

The waitress in the café noticed the three of them immediately, and approached to offer them a table. It was Clara, the waitress they had gotten to know from their various visits here. Clara recognized them, and recognized Leopold too. She greeted them with a pleasant smile, and soon brought them cups of hot coffee with cream. While she took down Thomas' order of toast and eggs, she noticed Leopold sitting patiently underneath the table, eyes looking up at her as if expecting her to take down his order as well.

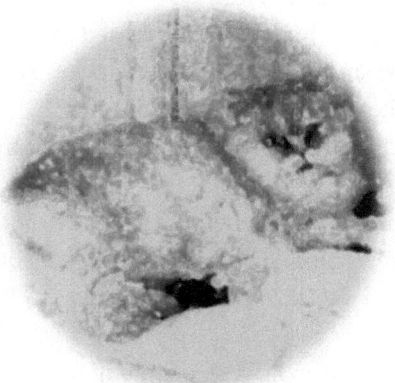

"Well, Leopold, I have something special for you too," she said, and then ushered towards the back kitchen to put in Thomas' order and fetch Leopold's special dish.

"Don't tell him, but I think this cat is spoiled," Betty murmured softly, and earned a smile from Thomas in reply.

"He's well-adored," Thomas responded, and then took a sip of his coffee.

Betty took a sip from her cup in turn, relishing the warmth and strong taste as much as the scent. The coffee aroma still reminded her a bit of her father. Thinking on this in the moment, she remarked, "I do like coffee. You know, my father had an idea to expand The Sapphire Key and add a coffee shop."

"Oh, really?" Thomas replied. "He decided not to go through with it, I assume."

"I'm not really sure," Betty responded, suddenly realizing that there had never been a conversation about expanding the shop. She did know, however, that a coffee shop had been part of Henry's initial vision for the building that he had transformed into the bookshop. "It was never *decided*, in the full sense of the word. But it is something he had wanted to do," Betty explained.

"Well, for what it's worth, I think it's a good idea," Thomas remarked.

Betty raised her eyebrows. "You do?"

"Sure. You have the Reading Room there, with coffee tables. It would sure be convenient if folks could get their coffee or tea in close proximity. And a benefit to *you*, as well." He meant that a coffee shop could result in an additional stream of income for Betty. Thomas' words made sense to her, and it *was* beginning to sound like a good idea. It would take planning, of course, but there was no rush and the necessary preparations could be made.

"Thanks. It's definitely something I'll think about," she said, with a tone that was thoughtful.

As Thomas nodded, the waitress Clara returned with two

plates. One held Thomas' order of toast and eggs, and the other carried the strong scent of tuna fish.

"Here you are, sir," Clara announced, placing Thomas' plate in front of him on the table. "And, here you are, Leopold."

The cat, who had clearly already been expecting her to bring him a treat, sat on the floor by Betty's feet, licking his lips in anticipation. With a chuckle, Clara presented him with the plate of tuna, and, after thanking her with a meow, Leopold began eating heartily.

The three enjoyed their breakfast, and Betty and Thomas chatted idly while they finished their coffee and waited for Clara to return to take their plates and present the bill. Betty glanced around, noticing that more customers were coming in, and she commented to that effect. Her gaze then fell again on the gentlemen she had noticed when they first arrived. He had placed the newspaper down so that it no longer obscured his face. Betty was startled to realize that she recognized him. It was Mr. L.J. Simpson. Betty had not seen him come into town for a good while, and had never seen him at this café. He was a bit of a town celebrity, and ordinarily would be surrounded by a throng of people heading up some event with a great deal of fanfare. It was a nice change to see him in this environment.

At that moment, Clara returned to their table and Thomas took the bill from her. Betty looked at Clara and commented softly, "I see that Mr. Simpson is here having breakfast."

"That's correct," Clara replied. "Apparently, he couldn't sleep, so he decided to come down early to the café."

Betty nodded and glanced over once more to see Mr. Simpson rising from his seat, leaving the newspaper behind, and exiting the café.

Betty looked back at Thomas and muttered, "What is it about today that everyone could not sleep and rose early?"

Thomas smiled and handed the bill back to Clara along with the payment for their meal. "Sometimes you have to get up early to find things out. To catch the worm, as the saying goes."

"Hmm," Betty replied, smiling at Thomas' analogy, and at Leopold's answering meow. She wondered what she was supposed to find out today.

C3

The three made their way back to The Sapphire Key, and still it was well before the time that the shop usually opened for business. Betty opened the door and was surprised to see the lights inside already on, and Elizabeth standing at the counter. Betty knew then that Elizabeth had also been unable to sleep and had risen early.

"Well, it's an early start for all of us," Betty greeted. At this point, it really came as no surprise that everyone around Betty had risen early too. Further, at this rate, customers could start coming in before the usual opening time. It was a good thing, then, Betty supposed, that she and Elizabeth would be ready to receive them.

Betty and Thomas said hello to Elizabeth, gave a brief recounting of their breakfast at the café and their sighting of Mr. Simpson, and then Thomas prepared to go on his way back to the inn, where he planned to catch up on some reading and editing.

Just as he waved goodbye and headed towards the front door, Betty noticed Leopold at his feet and leaving with him. She did not mind it, as she expected that the cat only wished to say goodbye to Thomas. However, as Thomas walked further down the street, Leopold continued to walk alongside him.

Betty told Elizabeth that she would be right back, and then exited the door herself, calling out, "Leopold!"

Thomas turned at the sound of her voice, and looked down to see the cat at his feet. "Sorry, Betty—I didn't realize that he was still following me." He bent down to rub the cat behind his ears, and said, "All right, then, you better get on back." Thomas stood back up, gave another wave to Betty, and resumed his walk. Still, the cat continued to follow him. Thomas turned around and shrugged. "Maybe he wants a walk," he offered. "Don't worry, he'll stay with me, and I'll walk back with him at lunch."

With a slightly exasperated look at Leopold—he was going to be a troublemaker today, by his behavior—Betty nonetheless assented to this plan, thanked Thomas, and went back inside of the shop. As she did so, placing her belongings on the counter, Elizabeth raised her eyebrows and said, "So, you couldn't sleep, either?"

⊂⊰

Within the hour, Betty and Elizabeth had prepared the shop for the day and completed a bit of filing work leftover from the day before. As Betty glanced out of the window, she saw that it looked to be a cool and cloudy day, though there was also a bit of smoke in the sky. Betty found this to be slightly unusual, but supposed it was coming from the lumbermill or the neighboring factories.

She thought nothing more of it until she and Elizabeth were interrupted by the sound of the North Bend fire engine rumbling down the road. They glanced at each other and then rushed to the door to see what was happening. As they looked out the door, they indeed saw the REO fire engine[6] driving down the street, followed by several cars which Betty assumed seated some of the North Bend firemen.

"What is happening?" she asked aloud, and then, when she stepped out into the street, she saw it. Smoke billowing up into the air, coming from the direction of the local inn, where Thomas was staying. "Oh my," she gasped, and at the same time, Elizabeth was already grabbing their coats. They spoke no more words to each other, but there was no question that they were going to the inn. If there was a fire at the inn, as they suspected, and Thomas and Leopold were inside of the inn...

People from all around them were coming out to take a look. If others in town were not already awake, they certainly were now. Betty was starting to feel the sharp pain of anxiety in her chest. They were moving quickly, but still her feet could surely not carry her quickly enough. What if they did not arrive in time?

As if the universe had heard her thoughts, a car pulled alongside them, and a familiar voice rang out to her.

"Betty! What are you doing? Haven't you heard there's a fire? Get in."

Betty and Elizabeth stopped in their tracks. Clarence Highley had pulled his car to the side of the road beside them. As was his tendency, he had arrived just in time to assist her. Looking over at him gratefully, Betty complied and stepped into the backseat of the car, helping Elizabeth to come in beside her.

---

[6] The REO Motor Car Company manufactured cars, trucks, and other automobiles. Its 1920 fire engine was the first of its kind that included a pressurized system to expel water. It was able to hold 150 gallons of water. See the book *North Bend* by Dick and Judy Wagner for more information (Arcadia Pub., 2010).

"Oh, Clarence," Betty breathed. "It looked like smoke was coming from the inn. Can you drive there?"

Clarence turned around to look at her with incredulity in his eyes. "You're mad. It's too dangerous. Paul is on his way there now." Paul was one of the local firemen.

"Thomas and Leopold are in there," Betty replied emphatically.

Once Betty said this, and Clarence saw the fear in her eyes, he no longer argued with her, but revved the car and started driving as fast as he was able in the direction of the inn.

Elizabeth looked over at Betty and placed a reassuring hand on her arm. It felt useless to say anything like, "it will be okay," for one could never be sure such words would be true in a moment like this. Still, Betty appreciated the gesture and merely squeezed Elizabeth's hand in response.

They arrived at their destination in a few minutes, though it felt like the drive had taken an hour. Before Clarence or Elizabeth could stop her, Betty opened the car door and jumped out, all but running towards the entrance of the inn.

She was greeted with a chaotic scene. The fire engine was out front. A group of firemen assembled around it, and around the building, holding fire hoses that they propelled by hand to expel water. The firemen were easily identifiable by their uniforms, which had the large letters "NB" for North Bend embroidered on their vests and on their caps. A few worked at pumping water out from hoses, while others stood by the fire engine, which used its own pressurized system to produce water. Besides the team of firemen, a group of other people stood outside. Many were dressed in nightclothes, so Betty supposed that they must be guests of the inn. She did not detect any active flames, but saw smoke continuing to rise into the sky. In the noise and chaos, it was impossible to know where the smoke originated from.

"Betty!" Clarence had finally reached her, Elizabeth at his side. He gently took her arm. "Betty, I know you're worried, but you really shouldn't be…"

She looked at him with a hard expression. "I have to find them."

Clarence stalled for a moment, and said, "I see Paul over there. I'll ask if he's seen them." Without waiting for her reply, he ran towards one of the firemen.

Betty looked at Elizabeth, who also had fear in her eyes. Betty sighed, and said, "I'm sorry. I'm just…"

Elizabeth shook her head and pulled Betty into an embrace. "I know," she murmured. "Me too."

Betty let out a breath as Elizabeth released her, and the two stood for a quiet moment as if to reassure one another. Clarence soon returned to them. He did not speak right away, and gave a soft shake of his head. Betty knew then that Paul had not found Thomas or Leopold.

Clarence seemed to know that he would be unsuccessful if he tried to stop her, so he allowed Betty to go.

As she walked through the crowd, tears started to fill her eyes. She did not know if it was from the smoke or the feeling of increasing desperation that was rising in her chest. There were people everywhere, and she caught snatches of conversation like, "…from the side entrance…"; "…cigarettes…"; "…damage to the first-floor rooms…".

It was suffocating, and as she walked further, she felt like she might fall, right there, onto the ground. As her step began to falter, she felt a force against her back, stopping her. She soon realized that it was the arm of the fire chief. He was dressed in his fireman's uniform and jacket, with a protective helmet on his head. His face had a slight dusting of soot, but he was otherwise unmarred.

"Easy, Miss," he said, leaving his hand at her back to support her.

"Thanks," Betty replied. She had a creak in her throat from the smoke in the air. "I…" she started to attempt to explain herself, but the fire chief interrupted her.

"Your friend over there pointed you out. Said you were looking for someone."

Betty glanced behind him and saw Clarence standing a few paces away. Betty nodded.

"Well, I think I found who you're looking for," the fire chief said, and moved over a step. Behind him, standing on the side of the road, were two figures.

She saw them. Thomas and Leopold. They were safe and away from the smoke and chaos.

Before she could comprehend what the fire chief was saying next, she propelled herself forward and into Thomas' arms. His embrace felt strong and safe after the recent uncertainty. As he held her, and she felt Leopold's soft fur brushing against her legs, she realized how scared she had been and how utterly relieved she now felt in contrast.

She drew back and realized that Thomas was speaking to her.

"It's okay, I'm all right. We're both okay. We're not hurt. It was a small flame on the first floor. That's all. They've already put it out."

Betty slowed her breathing and registered what Thomas was saying. It took her a moment to find her words, and when she did, all she could say was, "Thank goodness you're safe."

"It was all Leopold," Thomas responded, as he continued to look at her intently.

Betty closed her eyes briefly and shook her head. "Leopold?" She then looked down at the cat. If he were not so big and bulky, she would like to hold him in her arms.

Thomas guided them to a bench, where they sat down. Leopold hopped up and curled onto Betty's lap with a loud purr. She stroked him gratefully.

"Yes," Thomas continued. "He followed me back here, and meowed the entire way. When we arrived, he continued meowing and stood in front of me." He paused and rubbed Leopold underneath his chin. His purrs grew louder. "It's like he wanted to stop me from going inside; to warn me."

Betty looked at Thomas with wide eyes. She was about to ask him what had happened next, when the fire chief approached.

"Miss, I see that you've found your person," the fire chief commented.

Betty smiled, looking over at Thomas, and glanced back at the fire chief with a nod. "Yes, thank you."

"Your cat here is something else," he continued, to Betty's surprise. "He was there at the fire station early this morning, making noise like you'd never heard, waking all of us up. A few of our men took a car down this way, and that's when they spotted the smoke. By that time, it was a small fire, and we were able to get the engine here in time to put it out."

Betty listened to the fire chief's explanation in quiet amazement. Leopold had been down to the North Bend fire station early this morning, and likely at four-o-clock. That explained why he had woken her up so early at five-o-clock. He must have jumped out of her bedroom window. Betty was in the habit of leaving the window open just enough so that Leopold's body could comfortably fit through. Apparently, he had just returned home from his excursion, which is why he made such a racket and awakened Betty. Leopold had awakened the firemen early as well, to alert them of an impending fire.

This was amazing to Betty, and confirmed her belief that

Leopold was no ordinary cat. She had always heard that dogs are naturally in tune with the weather, and could feel and smell changes in the air when a storm was brewing. Betty knew that some of the Coos Indians from North Bend believed that cats had some kind of magical power and intuition; that they too could sense inclement weather, but could also sense other impending situations. It was all very intriguing.

While these thoughts ran through Betty's mind, the fire chief continued explaining what had transpired. "…then, we arrive here to the inn, and see the cat again, meowing up a storm. It was the cat who pointed out the cigarette butts."

"What?" Betty finally replied. "Is that what caused the fire?"

"Well, Miss, it's hard to say. We don't know the cause of the fire for sure, so I can't say anything definitive. We did see several cigarettes by the side entrance of the inn, and that's where the flames were coming from." He paused and seemed to be preparing his words carefully. "It's hard to prove these things. We've seen a lot of fires in these parts caused by cigarettes that aren't put out."

Betty did not reply, as she was deep in thought pondering what the chief had said. It was Thomas who thanked the chief for the information and for his time, and then commented that he could see Clarence and Elizabeth on their way towards them.

So, Leopold had been at the fire station this morning. Then, he had woken Betty up. Then, he had followed Thomas to the inn.

Betty continued to stroke the large, orange cat, feeling comforted by the feel of his steady breathing and rumbling purr beneath her hand. But she also felt something akin to wonderment. Was it possible that Leopold had known about, or suspected, the fire?

Betty was left with these unfinished thoughts as Clarence and Elizabeth joined them. She would need to keep these thoughts to herself, and knew that it would be for the best. She gazed at Leopold and gave him an extra squeeze in gratitude before he hopped down as she and Thomas stood. Betty was soon in the midst of more embraces as the four of them exchanged exclamations of relief.

⚃

The rest of the morning was a blur, but they finally all climbed into Clarence's car and made their way back to The Sapphire Key. It was with surprise that they found people waiting there for them.

As they entered through the front door, they were instantly showered with attention from Betty's mother, Bea; Elizabeth's mother, Margaret; and Mrs. Alice Highley and her husband, John. After assuring them that they were all right, and that no one was harmed, they ceased asking questions. However, Mrs. Highley insisted that they all sit down and rest. She and Bea then took out canteens filled with hot coffee. Betty was not sure who, but someone had found or brought dixie drinking cups.[7] Before anyone could protest, they were all supplied with a cup of the steaming coffee as well as one of Bea's biscuits. Betty felt unable to drink or eat anything, but did so at Bea's insistence. She was surprised at how soothing the warm coffee felt against her throat. She assumed that Thomas, Clarence, and Elizabeth felt the same,

---

[7] The disposable "dixie cup" was popular in the 1920s, and the years following, to serve hot and cold beverages on-the-go. Post the 1918 Spanish influenza era, this disposable paper cup was preferred as a more sanitary option to prevent the spread of germs.

as she saw them sipping the coffee gratefully.

Soon, the topic of Thomas' accommodations came up. He could not remain at the inn now. The fire had not caused a large amount of damage, but guests were not allowed to stay due to exposure to smoke. Even after the smoke had cleared, repairs needed to be made on the first floor. Thomas needed another place to stay.

It was Mrs. Highley who first offered that Thomas stay in the guest bedroom of the Highley house. Her husband, John, and Clarence backed this idea immediately. Out of all other possible options, staying with the Highleys was likely the best. The Highley house had a second level of guest rooms, and they were in the custom of welcoming guests to stay with them. It was still in town, so Thomas would not need to travel to North Bend. As far as Mrs. Highley was concerned, it was decided.

Thomas either agreed with their reasoning, or was simply too tired to argue. Either way, he relented to this plan.

By the evening, he had moved his belongings to the Highley residence.

By the evening, Betty had found out many things. One of them was that she had a remarkable cat.

Chapter 6

Dinner Plans

They all slept in the following morning. The town seemed to be off to a slow start as news of the small fire at the local Marshfield Inn spread. The fire was reported in that week's paper. The story talked about how the firemen arrived at the inn just in the nick of time to prevent the flames from spreading. The cause of the fire was listed as unknown. The Inn was one of the buildings standing in the Coos Bay area constructed entirely from wood, making it especially susceptible to fire. As reported in the newspaper, the threat of fire in Marshfield and surrounding cities had been substantial in the recent years. Just in the last decade, the number of buildings destroyed by fires was astounding. One of their mills had burned down, which was devastating enough, in addition to other hotels and wood-constructed businesses. As Betty read this summary, she recalled that it had not been until just last year, 1919, that the City Council had approved the use of the REO fire engine to put out fires.[8]

Betty closed the newspaper, folded it, and put it away on a shelf in the storage room. It would soon become one of the accumulated memories in that room that Betty would reflect on in years to come. For now, she was ready to place it aside and move on to other things.

Thomas was ready to move on, too. He had relocated to the second-floor guest room of the Highley residence and acclimated quickly. He got along well with everyone, so it

---

[8] Wagner, Dick, and Judy Wagner. "Introduction." *North Bend*, Arcadia Pub., 2010, pp. 7–10.

was unsurprising that he struck up a friendship with Clarence. The day after the fire, they decided that they would all (Thomas, Clarence, and Samuel Clarkson) make wooden toys at the lumbermill over the weekend. The fire had not waylaid that plan, as far as Thomas was concerned. Mrs. Highley was against it, however, and Clarence and Thomas were only able to convince her after promising to be looked at by a doctor to check for signs of smoke inhalation. This seemed to assuage her motherly worry. Once they had seen the doctor and were cleared, Mrs. Highley could find no other reason to prevent the men from going.

Betty could understand Mrs. Highley's concern, for Bea held the same concern for her. Betty agreed to see a doctor as well, and also took Leopold to see a veterinarian. They were both cleared, which eased Bea as much as it eased Betty. This caused the return of a sense of calm to both the Featherwin and Highley households, and it was at this moment that Betty had decided to broach the topic of dinner to Bea. Happily, Bea was in favor of hosting. Most dinner parties were hosted by the Highleys, and Bea was glad of the opportunity to host a dinner herself for a change. Instead of inviting just Samuel and Edith, Bea insisted that Betty also invite the Highleys. This made perfect sense, and Betty had been planning to do so all along, especially since Thomas was now their guest.

Betty also felt that she wanted a way to thank Clarence. He had always been a good friend, and Betty was grateful to him for driving her and Elizabeth to the inn so quickly and enlisting the help of the fire chief to locate Thomas and Leopold. Clarence, being humble in nature, would deny that he did anything worthy of gratitude. Betty differed on this; his friendship meant a great deal.

Thus, it was decided that Bea would host the dinner on

Saturday evening after the men returned from their day at the mill. She would have all of the table place settings and dishes prepared.

Betty smiled softly. This was just the thing to get all of their minds off of the fire. In moments like these, it was good to be reminded of family and good friends.

❧

The remainder of the afternoon on Saturday passed by pleasantly. Betty had received a telegram that the order for the second shipment of T.Y.L.'s book had been processed, meaning that she could expect the books to arrive in two weeks. Meanwhile, the December issue of McClure's magazine came in early. That, at least, could occupy customers for the time being. As Betty flipped through the magazine, she came across the next installment of Zane Grey's *Wanderer of the Wasteland*. She recalled her conversation with Elizabeth several months ago about the author, and their speculation about whether the story would become a major publication. She placed a marker in the magazine and made a mental note to talk to Thomas about it later. She had intended to raise the topic with him long ago, but they had been distracted by other matters and it slipped her mind. For good measure, she wrote a note to remind herself. At some point during the dinner party or afterwards, she should have a chance to bring it up.

At the moment, though, Betty was wondering how the woodworking was going. It was just two-o-clock, so the men would be finishing up by now. She smiled, thinking again of her own wooden toy carvings at home, and eager to see what the men had made. It was now mid-November, which brought them closer to the winter holidays. She was surprised just how quickly this year had progressed, and how many changes and surprises had come about. She would not dare to venture a guess as to what the next month, and the next year, would bring.

☙

As early evening fell, with Bea, Betty, and Leopold inside of the Featherwin house preparing for the dinner, there was a sense of anticipation and excitement in the air—the same sense that Betty always had before a special gathering of people she cared about. Gatherings were plentiful among their circle in Coos Bay; regardless, Betty enjoyed each and every one. Bea, likewise, savored these gatherings, though perhaps enjoyed the preparation aspect more so than the actual event. It was a blessing that Bea was so skilled at cooking and decorating (and prided herself on those skills), for Betty still had much to learn from her in the way of homemaking. One day, she would be a good cook, seamstress, and hostess. For now, she was content to watch Bea and Mrs. Highley shine in those roles and set an example for others.

"Betty, would you set out the place settings?" Bea called to Betty from the kitchen, where she was cooking the types of foods that caused the most enticing aroma to waft through the house.

Betty finished folding the last of the freshly-laundered dinner napkins, which she then placed into a woven basket, and walked them into the kitchen. She was eager to see what Bea had prepared so far, and she was not disappointed.

The dining room was fit for a party. The deep myrtle draw leaf table shined and gleamed, and the matching chairs were spaced apart just so and adorned with white chair cushions. A table runner lay perfectly centered on the table top. It had been a gift from Ruth Smithson, and Bea habitually dressed the table with it for dinner parties. Ruth had hand-stitched it, and it was indeed a testament to her beautiful talent: the cloth was ivory in color, with small, burgundy flowers in the center and navy-blue stitching on the edges. The table was sufficient as-is for six guests, and the draw leaf mechanism—in which two "leaves" lay underneath the table top and could be extended out to give the appearance that the table was longer—allowed for a total of eight guests. This would accommodate their party nicely. Bea had already pulled out the leaves to extend the table, and had started the place settings. Each guest would sit before a lace placemat, on top of which sat a white porcelain plate. On one side of each plate was a porcelain bowl, and on the other was a crystal drinking glass. The only remaining place setting that Betty needed to arrange was the cutlery. She did so swiftly, finding the utensils waiting for her upon the library table, and then stood back to admire the result. The room looked lovely and inviting, though something was missing. In a moment, she realized what it was. Going to the cupboard in the kitchen, she fetched three cranberry candles. She set the candles an equal distance apart and the difference was immediate. The candles, whose deep burgundy color matched the flowers stitched upon the table runner, completed the room splendidly.

Bea appeared in the dining room just then, with a basket of fluffy, warm biscuits in her hands. She looked at Betty with a smile and an approving eye, and Betty knew that she was pleased.

Betty helped Bea find a place on the table for the basket, and then followed her into the kitchen to assist with remaining food preparations. Bea had cooked a wonderful dinner of chicken and potato-leek soup, and had cut up cabbage and carrots drizzled with a sweet cherry sauce. She had also baked a white cake topped with white icing and finely chopped nuts to enjoy after dinner with hot tea. Betty well-recognized this meal, for Bea had made it for her father often while he was alive. It made Betty happy to see Bea prepare it again with such love and care.

Just before their guests were due to arrive, Betty lit the cranberry candles, and also lit several kerosene lamps to brighten the house. The aroma of the food was all through the house now, and even extended to the front porch. It was evening, and the sky was dark, but the stars and street lamps were bright. So too were the smiles on the faces of their guests as they approached the Featherwins' porch. They would make an exact party of eight: Betty and Bea would be joined by Thomas Erwinshire; Samuel and Edith Clarkson; and Mrs. Alice, Mr. John, and Mr. Clarence Highley. Leopold the cat would be in attendance too, of course, though he had his own place in the kitchen to enjoy his special meal of canned salmon.

Betty stood on the porch, eager to greet everyone. Thomas was the first to arrive, followed closely by the Highleys. He looked dapper in a dark blue suit. When he reached the porch, he dipped his head in greeting and paused to take in the ambience and aroma. Then, looking at Betty with a smile, he said, "Can I eat now?"

Betty laughed, allowing him to take her hand as he met her at the door. "Soon enough, Mr. Erwinshire," she replied, and ushered him inside.

She stayed to greet the Highleys next, who were all in high spirits. Samuel and Edith arrived by car shortly thereafter, having come down from North Bend. As usual, Edith was as radiant as a beacon of light, and Samuel (still as smitten with her as the day he first met her) remained proudly by her side.

Once everyone was inside and at their seats, the dinner commenced. It was a perfect evening, enjoyed by all. Bea was so pleased to have visitors and pleasant conversations. Betty was sure that this would be only the first of many gatherings to come.

ogg

Later on, Bea and Mr. and Mrs. Highley retired to the parlor, with a sleepy and content Leopold joining them. Meanwhile, the young people (Betty, Thomas, Clarence, and the Clarksons) adjourned to the kitchen to enjoy their slice of cake and tea. Betty and Edith immediately asked about the men's day at work at the lumberyard. Edith had known of Samuel's hobby and was happy to boast of his talent and good heart to the group. This may have embarrassed humble Samuel a bit, for the tips of his ears turned rosy.

"It's become a tradition, really. And it puts all of us at the mill in the holiday spirit," Samuel said in response to his wife's compliment of his work.

Clarence nodded in agreement. "Yes, and it's a tradition that has spanned many years, if memory serves." He looked over at Betty, who acknowledged his statement.

"You and your father were working at the mill before I was old enough to be around the machinery," Betty said fondly. Clarence was eleven years her senior and had followed in his father's footsteps, taking up work at the lumbermill. Jobs at the mill and shipyards had been plentiful over the last decade, and still were, and offered good pay and benefits to the workers. All of the men that Betty knew who worked there—including her father—took pride in their work, and never wasted good wood scraps if they could help it.

Clarence smiled at Betty's words, likely remembering the times when young Betty visited the mill with her father, Henry. Those were the times when Henry, John Highley, and Clarence Highley had worked alongside each other, and had each spent time crafting gifts out of surplus myrtle wood to bestow upon the local children at Christmastime. Now, a decade later, Thomas, Samuel, and Clarence were keeping the same tradition alive.

"I remember. Though that didn't stop you from coming around, and working at the mill in turn," Clarence replied. He referred to Betty's work as the lumbermill desk clerk, which she had started when she was not yet seventeen. Even then, she had been eager to take up work and follow in Henry's footsteps.

"I was the desk clerk for a while," Betty explained, for Thomas' benefit, as he had not heard about Betty's job at the mill before, and listened to the conversation with interest.

"Who now owns the most profitable bookshop in Coos County," Edith offered with a bright smile. She had been in especially bright spirits, and full of complimentary remarks all evening. Her enthusiasm and support of Betty's endeavors warmed Betty's heart, and a slight blush appeared on Betty's cheeks.

"Thank you, Edith, though no doubt you exaggerate."

Everyone around her exchanged an almost imperceptible glance. It was true what Edith had said, as The Sapphire Key had done remarkably well in the two years now since Betty had taken full ownership. Betty was successful as a modern businesswoman, and everyone knew it—even Thomas. He met her eyes with his then, offering his own unspoken compliment to her.

Edith only smiled, and then returned to the topic at hand. "Well, tell us then—what did you create at the lumberyard? And how did you fare, Mr. Erwinshire?"

Thomas, of course, was not a lumbermill worker, and did not share the history that was embedded within Clarence and Samuel. Even so, he wore a subtle air of confidence that made Betty again suspect that he was more talented than he let on.

"Surprisingly well, for having not taken up woodwork in a while," he responded to Edith. "Though Clarence has the artist's touch. I am but a novice."

Clarence began to shake his head, though both Betty and Edith insisted that he could not deny Thomas' statement. They had both seen his work for sale in the general store and in Ruth Smithson's shop.

"We've started carving boats, and Samuel was working on a Model-T replica."

"Here, I've brought the start of one," Samuel added, and to Edith he said, "I knew you'd be wanting to see it."

He drew, from inside of his coat pocket, a wooden carving that could fit in one's hand. It was indeed in the shape of a car, carved from tan-colored myrtle wood. Samuel had shaped some pieces of wood into circles for the wheels. It was charming, and sure to be a favorite amongst the holiday shoppers.

"It's beautiful work," Edith commented softly, and the

others nodded. It was unclear who was the better artist—
Clarence or Samuel—and they had not seen Thomas' work
yet. When asked, Thomas replied that he had left his
unfinished project at the mill, and would be returning next
weekend to resume work on it. Betty had been keen on
seeing his handiwork, though was content to wait.

As they gradually moved to other topics, including
everyone's plans for Thanksgiving, Betty asked if they
would like any more of the cake. When all answered, "no,
thank you," Betty excused herself to wrap up the remaining
cake slices. Thomas accompanied her to the dining room to
assist with wrapping up the cake, and then returning it to
the icebox in the kitchen, near the pantry. Betty thanked
him, and was glad of the opportunity to speak with him
privately.

"How do you like your room at the Highleys'?" she
asked.

"Very well," Thomas replied. The Highleys'
accommodations exceeded those at the inn. "I'm grateful.
Mrs. Highley is generous, and I'm not sure how I'll repay
her."

Betty smiled. Mrs. Alice Highley was indeed a woman of
generosity, as was clear by her kindness towards Betty and
Bea when Henry had passed. "She knows that you
appreciate it."

"Still," Thomas responded, "I'll need to think of
something."

"Seeing as you're a skilled woodworker now, perhaps
you can fashion a wooden gift for her," she suggested
lightheartedly.

Thomas smiled. "Not a bad idea."

Her expression then shifted subtly, and her tone became
earnest. "Did you enjoy your time today? I know you

wanted to take your mind off of things."

Thomas nodded. "I did enjoy the day, and I think it did me some good." He paused for a moment, and then added, "It gave me time to reflect on the things that I'm grateful for."

Betty's eyes softened at this. Thomas did not expand on this, though he did not need to. "I'm glad," she replied. She was about to respond further, when Mrs. Highley approached them.

"Good evening, dears," she greeted. "I didn't have a chance to speak to you all evening, and wanted to remedy that." She smiled at them both. "I hope I'm not interrupting."

"Not at all," Betty assured her, and accepted her kind embrace.

"Your young man is an impeccable guest," Mrs. Highley said to Betty, referring to Thomas. "He's been helping out in the kitchen, and leaves everything in apple-pie order[9], which is a notch above John and Clarence."

Betty was not surprised to hear this, and found Thomas' humility endearing.

"It's the least I can do to thank you, Mrs. Highley."

"Tut, tut, we are pleased to host you. Now," she continued, and Betty could sense that she had something else she wanted to talk to them about. "How is your inquiry into the photograph going?" She referred to the photograph dated 1890 that she had given to Betty some months ago, of her sister, Sarah, standing with Thomas' mother, May. Mrs. Highley was the only other person in town, apart from Betty, who knew Thomas' backstory.

"Well, the woman next to your sister is definitely my

---

[9] Meaning, very tidy and well-organized.

mother," Thomas responded, and proceeded to tell her what he had told Betty already, about finding the other two photographs and linking them together by date. Mrs. Highley nodded while he explained, and commented that this was indeed good progress.

"The trouble is, we have very little else to go on," Betty interjected. "It seems that Thomas' mother may very well have known your sister, but beyond that, we can only speculate."

Thomas nodded, and then looked over to Betty inquiringly. Betty nodded back, and Thomas took this as encouragement to ask the question he next posed to Mrs. Highley: "Do you think your sister would remember my mother? We wondered if we could get in touch with her; whether it would be all right to send her a letter."

Mrs. Highley's eyes brightened, and she looked kindly at Thomas. "Oh, I'm sure it would be fine. I can't tell you if Sarah will remember your mother or not, but there's no harm in asking."

Both Betty and Thomas let out a breath of hope and relief.

"I'll place a call to her next week, to let her know to expect to hear from you. I won't say what it's about—I'll leave that to you."

"Thank you—that helps so much," Betty responded.

Mrs. Highley smiled. "I have her address, and I'll give it to you when we return home," she said to Thomas.

As Mrs. Highley turned towards her husband, who had called to her from the parlor, Betty and Thomas looked at one another. There was a sense of renewed hope in the air. Betty was just as eager as Thomas was to continue their search into May Bell Sebastian's life, and venture closer to the answers to their lingering questions.

Chapter 7

Zane Grey & McClure's

"I knew that she would be happy to help," Betty remarked to Thomas as Mrs. Highley returned to the parlor. They could hear the voices of Mr. Highley and Bea, chatting about the upcoming holidays and plans for hosting the next dinner. Traditionally, the Featherwins and Highleys rotated: Thanksgiving would be at the Highleys' while Christmas would be at the Featherwins', or vice versa. By the snippets of conversation that Betty could catch, it sounded as though the Highleys had offered their home for Thanksgiving. It was sure to be a topic of conversation next week, as the holiday was fast-approaching. Betty would be caught-up on the plans soon enough, and thus sought to tune out their voices as she returned her attention to Thomas.

"And I'm grateful. It's a bit odd, though."

Betty looked at him inquisitively. "What is?"

"A stranger writing to a stranger. I hope it won't seem…intrusive." Thomas seemed suddenly apprehensive about the plan to write to Sarah Mitchell, which was surprising given his earlier enthusiasm about it. Still, Betty could understand his hesitancy. To come closer to receiving information about his mother—information he had craved for so many years—was a significant step that he would need to prepare for mentally as well as emotionally.

Betty's gaze softened. "It must seem incredible to be so close to knowing more about your mother. But, remember that Sarah Mitchell is a mother too, and will surely understand your request. Mrs. Highley certainly did, and she supports you."

Thomas nodded and the line of concern on his forehead faded. "You're right, of course. I'm overthinking it."

Betty smiled. "It's all right. And you're not a stranger to her—not really. If you want, I can help you draft the letter."

Thomas looked relieved when she said this. "Thank you. Yes, I think I would like that."

"Good. It's decided then," Betty replied. They both turned towards the main kitchen area, from where they heard echoes of laughter. It sounded as though Clarence and the Clarksons were having a lively conversation.

Thomas smiled and suggested, "Perhaps we should rejoin them."

"Yes," Betty agreed, and glanced at her wristwatch. The hour was growing late, and soon Bea would be calling them all together. "Before we go…" Betty added, placing a hand on his arm to halt his steps. "I wondered if we could talk business for a moment."

Thomas paused, and turned back to her with a raised eyebrow. "Sure. What's troubling you?"

"It's nothing unfavorable," she assured him, and continued with a smile, "On the contrary, I wanted to let you know how grateful I am that you chose The Sapphire Key to debut T.Y.L.'s book. Sales from the first shipment of the books exceeded our expectations."

Thomas beamed. "I am glad to hear it. Mr. Lamore is not disappointed either," he responded, using T.Y.L.'s full last name. "And from what I hear from John, sales are high in Washington as well." His associate, John Noble, was overseeing the book showcase at a bookstore in Pasco just this week.

"I am not surprised," she said. Many authors did not experience such success so soon. However, it appeared that this author, largely unknown as of earlier in the year, was shooting towards stardom in record time. He had chosen the right genre and topic of writing at the right time.

Zane Grey was another author who had shot to prominence in the recent years.[10] This was who she wished to speak to Thomas about. She had made the note to herself to bring it up, and now was the opportunity.

"Also, I've been interested in another author's works," she continued. Thomas looked at her expectantly. "Are you familiar with *Wanderer of the Wasteland* by Zane Grey?"

A flicker of recognition lighted in Thomas eyes. "Yes, very familiar. It's been serialized in McClure's magazine this year."

"Yes, that's right. We keep the magazine in stock, and Elizabeth brought it to my attention. I've asked her to keep an eye on the reviews and future installments."

"That is prudent," Thomas replied. "It's looking like a success already. And, the fact that McClure's is continuing to print Grey suggests that the serial will be published in book form."

Betty nodded. This confirmed her, and Elizabeth's, assumptions.

"Additionally," Thomas continued, "it's likely to go to a larger publisher soon."

Betty frowned slightly, wondering at the meaning of this statement, and pressed Thomas on it.

---

[10] *See* Gross, Sarah Jane. "Chapter 9: Zane Grey." *The Two Secrets.* Sarah Jane Gross, 2020. Pearl "Zane" Grey was a real-life author who wrote romantic American western novels. By early 1920, he was a most popular and sought-after author, with lucrative offers from several magazines (including McClure's) to print his works. Recommended reading on Grey is *Zane Grey: His Life, His Adventures, His Women* by Thomas H. Pauly (University of Illinois Press, 2005).

Thomas lowered his voice a bit, hearing the others approaching, and murmured, "McClure's is changing."

Betty wanted to ask him further what he meant and continue their conversation, but did not have the opportunity. Before either Betty or Thomas could say anything further, Bea approached them and was closely followed by Clarence and the Clarksons. She wished to gather everyone into the parlor. This meant that the party was drawing to a close, and their conversation would need to be left there for now.

Giving in to Bea's request, Betty cast a remorseful glance at Thomas, and they all filed into the parlor to begin the round of "thank you's" and "goodbyes" before departing the Featherwin house for the evening. Bea supplied everyone with the leftover slices of cake, and Thomas then headed out with the Highleys while the Clarksons hopped into their car to drive to North Bend.

Once the house was quiet again (even Leopold was still snoozing on the hearth, tired after all of the attention), Betty agreed with Bea that the dinner had been very pleasant. Neither she nor Bea could have wished for a better one. In fact, Bea was in such good spirits that she told Betty not to worry about the rest of the dinner clean-up—they would get to it in the morning.

Betty was pleased that the dinner had gone so well, but did wish that she and Thomas had been able to finish their conversation. She still wondered at the implication of his statement—that McClure's magazine was changing—and was eager to resume the topic when she next saw him.

∞

The following Monday was a chilly one. Winter had made itself known with the recent rains and cold front, and was in Coos Bay to stay—at least for the next couple of months. Even now, the gray-white sky foretold of the snow that would fall and blanket the streets in a layer of frost. On the walk this morning to the bookshop, Betty noticed her breath creating pockets of condensation in the air. Yes, it would be a chilly winter.

She entered the bookshop with a contented sigh, pleased to be inside and amongst the paper and ink, stories and biographies, that made up the books surrounding her. Every morning when she stepped foot into her shop, she felt a sense of calm and belonging that she had never felt anywhere else. The Sapphire Key was her sanctuary, and she felt that, in a way, it was her purpose to make it a success and carry on her father's legacy. And maybe Henry Featherwin had ensured that she would. She pondered as her gaze fell upon the sapphire-blue lamps, and her mind's eye then drifted to the writing desk in the storage room, and the myrtle picture frame in the Reading Room. These items all carried a history of their own that would stay alive because of Betty, and their own secrets which Betty would keep safe.

It was her responsibility, and she took that seriously, which is why she remained grateful for the success of the bookshop. It was strange how much she missed being in the shop, even after one day's absence, and was glad to be back and onto the routine of a new week. She looked forward to assisting the day's customers. She equally looked forward to inquiring into Thomas' statements about Zane Grey and McClure's, which had not left her mind since the end of the party.

Thankfully, she did not need to wait long. Both Thomas

and Clarence came around within the hour—Clarence, on his way to the mill and Thomas, to inquire if he could work on some edits in the Reading Room. She was pleased to receive them. After seeing Clarence to his car (he would come by again later to collect Thomas), Betty gave her consent to Thomas using the Reading Room, and then joined Elizabeth at the counter to see to a customer.

The morning remained busy until the customer traffic diminished at around eleven-o-clock. Elizabeth seemed grateful for the pause in activity, and remarked, "I'm glad that we're busy, but I hope I can have a few moments of quiet now. I'd like to finish filing all of those receipts."

Betty nodded. She knew that Elizabeth liked a quiet environment to do that sort of detail-oriented work. "Well, if you'll be doing that, I'm going to pop into the Reading Room to check on Thomas."

Elizabeth nodded. She already had the folder of last week's receipts on the counter. Betty smiled, amused at her assistant's ability to refocus, and started to walk towards the back of the shop to the Reading Room. There, she found Thomas at work over a stack of papers, and Leopold lounging on the floor beside him. She smiled as she looked upon the scene through the door's glass panes. They were quite the pair, and Thomas appeared so engrossed in his task—glasses on the bridge of his nose, pen scratching annotations onto a page—that she was hesitant to interrupt him. As her hand touched the door handle, though, he must have sensed it, for his eyes met hers through the glass pane at the same moment. He dropped his pen and smiled, and she accepted the invitation in.

"I see that you're keeping busy, and you have Leopold for company," she remarked as she entered.

"He's a silent companion," Thomas replied, grinning as

the cat yawned and stretched and then tucked his face under a paw to go back to sleep.

Betty was careful to step around Leopold as she ventured to the center of the room. "I'm sorry to interrupt."

"No, I'm in need of a break," he insisted, and indicated that she should take a seat across from him. "This is an article sent over from John," he explained, referring to the associate from his office in Washington. "Edits have been done, but he asked for my final approval." By the way he described it, Betty could sense that it was somewhat of a demanding task. The numerous papers strewn across the table supported this guess.

"Can I help?" she offered.

"No-thank you," he said quickly, though smiled at her gesture. "Reviewing the article itself is fine, it's just the added pressure of doing it quickly to send back to the office." He sighed and added, "I'm wondering how efficient it is, and how long it can go on like this. But, no matter. Tell me—what's on your mind?"

Betty did not answer him right away. She was concerned about what he had just said, and it made her wonder too. Thomas had made arrangements to stay in Coos Bay longer than originally anticipated, but she knew that those arrangements had to end at some point. She wondered, even now, how Thomas was able to manage matters for his office from afar. It was surely a strain, even if he did have help in his associate, John, and their new hire. A part of her wanted to ask him about his long-term plans, but the other part of her—the part that wished to remain in her present reality, with Thomas in Marshfield indefinitely—won out. She therefore did not question Thomas then, and neither did he expand upon it. The subject would come up again, but not today.

"I wanted to finish our conversation," Betty replied.

"Oh, yes. Zane Grey and McClure's," Thomas responded accurately. "He's quite popular now, so to have your eye on him is wise."

Betty nodded. "I thought as much when Elizabeth showed me his piece in the magazine." She eyed him inquisitively. "Now, what's this about McClure's?"

He was quiet for a moment. At length, he answered, "Well, I hesitate to repeat unconfirmed information, but as you keep McClure's in stock…"

Betty creased her brow, her interest piqued as she waited for him to continue.

"There's been talk of Grey in negotiations with other outlets over *Wanderer of the Wasteland*."

Betty eyes widened. "What do you mean?" She suspected that this meant that other magazines had approached Grey about publishing rights, but she asked anyway.

"I hear that Harper's[11] has been after him for quite some time, with consistently higher offers," Thomas replied in a soft voice.

Betty understood what this implied. *Wanderer* could soon be found in print in Harper's rather than in McClure's. Harper's was a much larger outfit, with deeper pockets, and could well-afford to pay a high price to obtain Grey.

By the change in Betty's expression, Thomas could likely tell that she had connected the dots. He continued, "And there's been a change in leadership at McClure's, and the accompanying shift in magazine style."

---

[11] Harper & Brothers was an influential magazine and book publisher in the 19th and 20th century. It is true that Harper's was in negotiations with Zane Grey to publish his books. For more history on this, recommended reading is the work by Thomas H. Pauly, cited in the previous footnote.

"Yes," Betty nodded. "I had noticed that."

"Now, I'm not saying any of this is for sure, but I thought you should know what's been brewing around the rumor mill."

"I'm glad that you've told me this," she replied, appreciative of his candor. She had recently been reviewing the bookshop subscriptions for the new year and McClure's came up as a question mark. Of course, given the unreliability of rumors, she would merely ask Elizabeth to keep an eye on sales of the magazine over the next few months and, perhaps, look into Harper's.

"Of course," Thomas replied, and then attempted to straighten the unruly stack of papers. The rustling noise that the papers made attracted Leopold's attention. Before either of them could intervene, Leopold flew, in a flash of orange, onto the table and began swatting at the papers enthusiastically.

"Oh, Leopold!" Betty chastised him, though could not resist a smile at his playful behavior. Thomas smiled too, and soon the both of them were laughing, and continued to do so even after Leopold had lost interest and hopped down to resume his place on the floor. He left behind an even messier stack.

"Here," Betty breathed, picking up several pages that had fallen to the floor, and tried to put the stack in order.

"Thanks," Thomas said, and joined Betty to partake in the clean-up. "I've never seen that cat be so disruptive."

Betty let out a short laugh. "You should have seen the state of my room when Leopold awoke me at five in the morning—books and bottles all over the floor." She smiled, but then her expression shifted. "That was the day of the fire."

Thomas took another page from her, and his own

expression changed as he regarded her. "We're lucky that Leopold warned all of us, as he did."

Betty returned her gaze to Thomas', seeing the compassion in his intense, hazel eyes, and knowing that, while she had been scared on that day, she need not be scared anymore. She simply nodded then, acknowledging his statement.

"I'll tell you what," he continued. "Let me finish up this review, then how about you and Elizabeth join me and Clarence for lunch?"

Betty brightened at this suggestion. "That would be lovely."

"Excellent."

೮೩

Betty left Thomas to his work, and passed the remainder of the morning tending to customers. By noon, they were all ready for lunch, and met Clarence at the nearby café for sandwiches. Betty was pleased to see that the men had, indeed, struck up a fast friendship, and both were pitching in to help Mrs. Highley. It was nice to have strong, reliable men around, and Thomas was fitting in nicely with the lumber boys. They all, collectively, carried Henry Featherwin's work ethic and spirit. Betty felt that, in an odd and marvelous way, Henry lived on through these men as much as through The Sapphire Key. The notion gave her a feeling of completeness that was difficult to explain, but could be felt.

೮೩

When they returned to the shop after the quick though enjoyable meal, Clarence lingered for a bit before returning to the mill. He remarked on how large Leopold had become. It was true—the cat appeared especially big now that his fur had grown out for warmth during these winter months. Such a stark contrast to the summertime, when Leopold was still large but his fur was much less dense. That is when Clarence had first found the cat wandering along the docks, and had dropped by the bookshop to see if Betty would take the cat in. The memory of that June day still brought a smile to Betty's face, and how much had changed since then!

Enjoying their reminiscence for a moment, Clarence then noticed the time and asked if Betty needed anything before he and Thomas headed out. She had a mind to say "no", but, for some reason, she thought of the writing desk in the storage room. When she asked whether they would be willing to help her move it into the Reading Room, they agreed to do it immediately.

They all made their way to the storage room, where Betty showed them the mahogany desk in the corner. Though the desk had seemed large and bulky to her, Thomas and Clarence pulled it out with seemingly no effort. As they did so, she was startled to see that it was still in good condition. Except for a thin layer of dust, the wood was unmarred. Even Thomas and Clarence seemed awed by its condition, and surprised that a useable piece of furniture would be hidden away.

"How long has this been in there?" Clarence asked as he took one end of the desk, while Thomas took the other. They slowly started to carry it out, careful not to nick any of the legs against the door.

"I'm not entirely sure," Betty responded, following them

out. "It was my father's."

"Ah," both men responded, understanding then that the desk had been in the storage room for at least two years, if not more.

"I'm glad you thought to take it out," Thomas remarked. "It's a beauty."

"It is," Betty agreed. As they moved it, her eyes fell across the intricate woodwork. She knew that the gold-flecked mahogany would glisten once she dusted it. Her eyes then alighted on the gold drawer handle, and she remembered what she had found inside of it: the receipt for the sapphire lamps. She had since locked the receipt away, and still was intent on keeping the lamps' true value a secret. It was for the best.

"All right—where would you like it?"

Betty quickly moved to open the Reading Room door for them, and gave the room a look-over to determine the most sensible spot. After a moment, she found it. There was space under the large window. She could scoot a chair there as well, later on, but even if she did not, the desk would look good there. It matched the wood on the glass cabinet, and seemed to compliment the room overall.

The men finished setting the desk in place with little effort, remarking how well it looked, and refusing to accept her thanks. As she admired the result, her eyes taking in the entire room, there was a moment in which she saw something that gave her pause. In a flash, like a vision or a memory, she saw the addition to the Reading Room that she had thought about before, but had never fully formed. She saw, to the right of the large window, another room that extended out. It was about the same size as the existing Reading Room, though had an open layout with wooden floors, several round tables, and a countertop. Behind the counter, on the wall, was a sign that read, "Sapphire Key Coffee." The letters were in the same shade of gold as the letters on the bookshop's front door. When she blinked, the image was gone.

೧

It was not until long after Clarence and Thomas had left, and the afternoon hours had passed, that Betty returned to the Reading Room with Leopold. She studied the window, and the writing desk underneath it, though saw nothing amiss. She then looked at the wall, where the threshold to a coffee shop might be.

"Do you see it?" she whispered to Leopold.

The cat looked at her with his bright green eyes, turned to look in the direction she was staring, and then meowed.

Betty was not sure whether to take his meow as a "yes" or a "no" this time, and resolved to put the strange imagining out of her mind. Still, she thought, as she bid Elizabeth goodnight and gathered her effects, there was something intriguing about the Reading Room and a sense of things to come at The Sapphire Key.

THE THIRD SECRET

Chapter 8

Thanksgiving

Thanksgiving was just around the corner, and as Betty expected, the holiday became a topic of conversation amongst all of the locals. It was a time when businesses would slow down as folks spent time with family and dear ones at home. The mill, shipyard, and factories would continue operations, but employees were always allowed the day (or, at the very least, a portion of the day) to focus on family time.

For Betty's part, she planned to close the bookshop for the day. If she did not, she would earn an earful from Bea. Family time during the holidays was non-negotiable for her, and increasingly, it was non-negotiable for Betty as well. When her father, Henry, had been alive, they always spent the holidays together in the house—just the three of them—and simply enjoyed each other's company. In those days, Bea would cook a quaint though hearty meal while Henry told stories, and Betty would listen and wonder where her father came up with his tall tales. This dynamic inevitably changed in 1918. After Henry's passing, nothing felt the same. Bea had lost all enthusiasm about the holiday and, for a while, it appeared that they would not observe their traditions at all.

Mrs. Highley turned this around. That year, she insisted that Betty and Bea join her family for Thanksgiving, and would not accept "no" for an answer. She had Clarence pick them up in his car on the morning of (just to make sure that they would not talk themselves out of coming), and showered them with tasks once they arrived at the Highley residence. They felt, truly, like part of the Highley family that day. Mrs. Highley took pains to ensure that they felt welcome, and kept Bea so busy with helping her in the kitchen that there was no time for her to realize that Henry was not with them. It was a brilliant strategy. Both Bea and Betty ended that Thanksgiving feeling as though their hearts were starting to heal—just a little bit—and that, perhaps, they could survive the rest of the year.

The Highleys' support meant a great deal to them during that trying time, and that November of 1918 marked the start of a new tradition. Ever since then, the Highley and Featherwin families celebrated the winter holidays together. It was a season Betty always looked forward to. It was a time when friends were treated like extended family; a time that served as a good reminder of all of the things to be grateful for.

This year, Betty was grateful for many things. In that spirit of gratitude, she thus set aside time in the evenings that week before Thanksgiving to spend extra time with Bea to chat about nothing and everything. It was the three of them this year—Betty, Bea, and Leopold—and while the void left from Henry's passing was not completely filled, Leopold's presence went a long way.

The days leading up to Thanksgiving found many others in a reflective mood as well. Samuel Clarkson was continuing to spend the weekends at the lumberyard crafting wooden toys, and had made great progress. He had made at least a dozen toy cars, and was in the midst of creating another "surprise" that he had not yet revealed. Thomas, too, had spent several more Saturdays at the lumberyard. The others (and Betty, especially) were curious about what he was working on, but he had not shown his work to anyone yet. Apparently, Thomas' projects would be a surprise too. Clarence, at least, was willing to share the results of his woodwork. He had made toy animals and boats from myrtle wood, and planned to showcase the charming collection at the general store in Marshfield and at Ruth Smithson's giftshop in North Bend. He planned to also set aside some toys especially for the local school children. Apart from the toys, Clarence had created a desk plaque with the words "Thank You" carved into the wood for the schoolteacher. He told Betty and Thomas that he would surprise the children with the toys, and the schoolteacher with the plaque, on their last day of school.

The sense of giving and gratitude was contagious, and similar acts of kindness could be found throughout the town: the grocer handing out produce, free of charge; the fire chief doing an extra check-up on the furnaces of local businesses; and the ice cream factory by the North Bend train station offering a complimentary scoop to passengers disembarking from return trains.

∞

It was in this spirit of appreciation that Betty, Thomas, and Clarence took the afternoon before the holiday to spend on the beach below the cliffs. Samuel and Edith would spend Thanksgiving with Samuel's family, the Clarksons, in North Bend. It would be a large turnout. They would drive up early to help with baking pies, setting the table, and anything else that needed to be done to prepare the Clarkson house for the holiday.

Meanwhile, at the lumbermill, a holiday meal would be provided for the workers. Those men who lived in the cottages at the mill were welcome to invite their extended family to the meal as well. It was an annual event held in the mess hall, and quite a spectacular one, with a surplus of comforting food and music to add to the merriment. Roasted turkey was always served, along with potatoes, butternut squash and sage soup, and cornbread. There were a great many pies delivered from the bakery as well. The North Bend local band played tunes in the hall during the meal, and this never failed to bring the workers to their feet to take a turn on the dance floor with their wives. It was a lovely gesture of appreciation to the mill workers. Everyone would end the day with a full stomach and a full heart, having enjoyed good food, good company, and good music.

While Clarence and his father had, on occasion, partaken in the lumbermill's Thanksgiving, they now habitually just spent an hour or two with the lumber boys for a small feast a couple of days before the holiday. The day before Thanksgiving, and the actual day itself, were spent in the Highley house for the family meal. If nothing else, the families in Coos County were known for their traditions, and it was a tradition of the Highleys to spend much of the day before Thanksgiving together at home baking pies and other desserts.

Another tradition was a visit down to the shore to watch the great, roaring waves crash against the cliffs. For Betty, this was an annual event. Although it was cold in November and December, she made a point of venturing down to the small and flat beach surrounded on both sides by a thick foresting of trees and the rugged cliff face. It offered a good vantage point to observe the waves crashing against the rocks that protruded above the water's surface. With a view of the Simpson estate above, it was fittingly known as "Simpson Beach."

The high tides in November created a dramatic and picturesque scene. After each crash, the waves would draw back into the sea and leave seashells and various rocks behind in their wake. Betty had collected many shells over the years. The waves were in constant motion, and the ocean breeze was fine and misty. There was a wide area of flat rocks upon the sand where Betty (and others who likewise enjoyed this tradition) would sit and enjoy this display of nature's beauty.

On this day before Thanksgiving, Betty decided to stop by the Highley house to see if Thomas and Clarence would like to join her at the shore. It was still early, and there was plenty of light in the sky.

As she approached, Clarence was already on the porch as if he had been expecting her. He leaned on the porch rail, and his sleeves were rolled up to his elbows in the way of someone who had been working with their hands. The breeze in the air carried the scent of just-baked scones as she drew nearer to the house, and she assumed that Mrs. Highley had been in the kitchen, as expected. She looked at him with a smile and greeted, "Why, hello there."

"Hello, Betty," he replied, and extended a hand to indicate that she was welcome to ascend the steps up onto the porch.

"Your mother has been baking?"

"She has," Clarence acknowledged. "And you're on your way to the shore."

Betty grinned. She did not ask how he knew this, but instead responded, "We do have our traditions, don't we?"

Clarence nodded, and then asked, "So, what brings you by?"

"I wondered if you and Thomas wanted to join me. Thomas has never been to that part of the beach, and I thought it would be nice if we took him." She paused to gauge his reaction, and then added, "We won't stay long, as it's cold. What do you think?"

Clarence appeared to be in favor of the idea by his pleased expression, and answered, "Your timing couldn't be better. I was just telling Thomas, actually, about your habit of visiting the shore just before Thanksgiving and Christmas."

She raised her eyes inquiringly, and he continued, "I'd love to come, if Mrs. Highley will release me." He said these words in jest, referring to his mother who was still busy inside with meal preparations. "Here," he added, opening the door. "Come on inside. I'll fetch Thomas and let mother know that we're going. I think it's a good idea to show Thomas the beach, and it's a good way to end the day."

With that, he left her in his front parlor for a few moments as he descended the hall towards the large kitchen area. Betty could hear their voices, and the house already had the warm and comfortable feeling of the holidays. She anticipated that tomorrow would be enjoyable for everyone. Before she could linger much longer with these thoughts, the two men came walking towards the parlor.

"Mother says to have a nice time, but to be back before dinner," Clarence reported.

"Very well," Betty replied with a bright smile, and turned to greet Thomas.

"We'll just gather our coats then, and be off," he said.

In a few moments, all three of them were dressed and ready (Betty was already bundled in her overcoat, gloves, and wool hat) and started on their way. En route, Betty told Thomas about the beach, which lay somewhat hidden and beneath the Simpson estate above. Besides the clifftop itself, the beach was one of the best and favorite spots to observe the shoreline and movement of the sea.

When they arrived, they saw several others standing upon the sand. They waved, and then went to enjoy their stroll and leave these beachgoers to enjoy their pre-holiday visit. Betty found a few seashells to add to her collection, and even Thomas stopped to pick up some small silver and jade-colored rocks.

Clarence joined them, selecting a white rock himself, and said to Thomas, "Not only does the sea offer an amazing display of the waves, but it also leaves us gifts."

Thomas laughed, and replied, "Indeed, it does."

Betty looked over at them curiously, surprised that Clarence was a collector of rocks and shells too, but also pleased that the men were getting on so well.

CB

They watched the waves for a little while and then departed the beach and returned to the Highley house feeling invigorated. Thomas offered to walk Betty home. It was a short walk, and Thomas told Clarence that he would be back in time for dinner. Betty accepted his offer with an expression of thanks, gave a quick wave to Clarence, and then she and Thomas started down the street.

"That's a beautiful spot—thank you," he murmured, as they walked.

"Of course," Betty replied. "We don't go to the beach nearly enough, but it is a nice thing to do at the holidays." She was quiet for a moment, and then said, "I think you know much of our holiday traditions already, but I know none of yours. How did you spend your last Thanksgiving?"

Thomas looked over at her and briefly replied, "With my cousins, the Erwinshires."

"Ah." She should have guessed that, she thought, and waited for him to expand on his statement.

At length, he did, but it was not with a recounting of enjoyable times, as she would expect. "It was not spent as pleasantly as yours," he said. Noticing the inquiring look in Betty's eyes, he proceeded to explain. "I wouldn't say that Violet and I had fallen out, but our relationship wasn't the same. We came together as a family and had a cordial meal, but Violet and I barely exchanged words."

Betty nodded, feeling saddened by his account. Violet Erwinshire was Thomas' aunt, but Thomas had thought of her as his mother for much of his adolescent life. As Thomas had recounted to Betty some months ago, he had learned of his true parentage when he was twelve years old. Only recently, he had asked Violet about his mother and father. Apparently, Violet had been unhelpful and unresponsive, which caused a rift to form between them. Even now, the Erwinshires were tight-lipped about Thomas' parents. It was, therefore, not completely surprising to Betty that Thomas' last holiday with the Erwinshires had been somewhat cold. It was not right, though, she felt, for the Erwinshires to be so dismissive towards Thomas when he was like a son to them. It was not her place to have an opinion, she knew, and so she kept these thoughts to herself.

She thus did not comment on it, but instead said, "I have a feeling that you'll have a pleasant holiday this year. Mrs. Highley would allow for nothing less."

Thomas smiled at this. True to form, Mrs. Highley had welcomed Thomas into her family's traditions, just as she had welcomed Betty and Bea two years before. Thomas was as good as family, and they were all rather looking forward to Thanksgiving. It had been decided that the Highleys would host, and that their "extended family" (meaning Thomas, Betty, Bea, and Leopold) would attend.

"I agree with that," he responded at length, with a laugh. "I'm very pleased to spend it with all of you." He stopped as they reached the Featherwin porch, and then allowed her to ascend the porch steps before him. He appeared to be deep in thought as he watched her take the steps, and said, finally, "It's funny, actually."

Betty leaned her hands on the railing and tilted her head inquisitively. "What's funny?"

"That it feels like home here, in a way I never expected."

She looked at him then, and noticed the shade of hazel in his eyes changing, and something else glimmer in his eyes as well. It gave her a strange feeling that she could not quite describe, but it was something close to happiness.

"It makes me glad to hear that," she responded softly.

"I've thought a lot about family," he continued. "As I have done for a while now. And, I'm ready to write that letter to Mrs. Highley's sister, Sarah."

"Are you, really?" Betty asked hopefully.

"Yes," he replied. "I think I know what I want to say, and I've grown more curious as to what she might have to say as well."

With those words, they both felt a stirring of something good to come, and would have been content to start writing the letter then and there. The clock was ticking, however, with Thomas due to return to the Highleys' for dinner, and he said goodbye. Tomorrow would be enjoyably spent, and there would be time later to be thoughtful and caring about the letter they would draft to Sarah Mitchell. For now, Betty was happy to close the door on this day, on this moment, and to open another door full of possibilities tomorrow.

Chapter 9

Changing Tides

The day of Thanksgiving passed by in a lively blur of food, family, and festivity. The traditional meal at the Highleys was spectacular, as expected, with all of the dishes and fixings that one could imagine on the table. Apart from partaking in the meal, they all spent the latter part of the day relaxing and chatting in the parlor. Leopold had his fill of turkey and of attention, and was therefore more content than Betty had ever seen him be. He did love being around people, and took time to visit with everyone before finding a snug spot by the Highleys' hearth to snooze. Thomas also seemed content, and Betty was glad to see it. After hearing his account of last year's Thanksgiving, she wished for him to feel part of their community; part of their family. Seeing how he smiled and laughed with Clarence, and how he was welcomed into the conversations, gladdened her, and made her feel that her wish had been granted. Betty was pleased to see Bea happy as well. When the festivities ended in the evening, everyone felt that the day had been a success. They headed home with two pieces of pie that they would eat later that night.

No sooner had Betty, Bea, and Leopold departed from the Highleys that plans for Christmas were already underway. These winter months always seemed to pass by too quickly for Betty's liking. There was much to do, from planning activities to preparing the menu, and the mood of Thanksgiving shifted swiftly. From feelings of gratitude sprung sentiments of joy. The school children were on break from their lessons, and were now seen all over town, shopping with their parents or playing in the gazebo in the town square. The children were so carefree in their play; just one look at them and it was quite impossible to feel anything except joy. The open-air bus was running this time of year as well to take passengers between Marshfield and North Bend. It was a fun mode of transportation that even Bea enjoyed for a change of pace.

Betty enjoyed this time too, especially the spirit of happiness and changing tides that could be felt in her bookshop. She liked to decorate the shop in December with a cheerful window display, and other odds and ends throughout. She usually did this on her own, though this year she was happy to have Elizabeth's help and input.

⚬

On December first, the week after Thanksgiving, Betty and Elizabeth were at the bookshop. They stood side by side, considering what to include in the shopfront window as a winter display.

Their initial thought had been to adorn the window in blue ribbons and cut-outs of snowflakes, and to tie the display to a winter-themed book. This was a great idea—if only they had a winter-themed book in stock! Elizabeth spent some time perusing the fiction shelves with no luck.

This is what led them to stand before the window now, discussing what might be both festive and beneficial in encouraging customers to come in. After exchanging half-formed ideas for a few minutes, Leopold interrupted them with a loud "meow" and hopped onto the windowsill himself. They laughed, amused at the sight of his large, orange body pressed against the windowpane. Then, Betty suddenly had an idea. Without saying anything else to

Elizabeth, she turned to go to the children's section of the Fiction bookshelf. There, she pulled several copies of *The Tale of Tom Kitten* by Beatrix Potter, a pleasant story that was a dear favorite of the local children. [12] She also pulled a lithograph of a painting from the storybook which depicted three striped kittens frolicking in a flower garden. She walked back to the shopfront window, encouraged Leopold down, and placed the books and lithograph on bookstands. She then stood back a pace to rejoin Elizabeth and inspect her work.

"Interesting choice," Elizabeth remarked. "But I think we should move this in the middle." She went over to the window to rearrange the placement of the books and lithograph, moving the lithograph to the center of the display and placing the books around it. "That way, it's like a centerpiece," she explained. "It will draw the customer's eye."

Betty smiled approvingly. "Good idea. Leopold, what do you think?"

The large orange cat, who had been watching them, turned his green gaze towards Betty and made a chirruping noise that sounded very much like he approved of the display as well. Betty laughed, and knelt down to stroke his head fondly, then said, "I think it's also time that I take out the box."

Elizabeth looked at her quizzically. "The box?"

Betty just smiled and asked Elizabeth to follow her to the storage room. This room, of course, stored all manner of odds and ends including a large hatbox. When Betty led Elizabeth to the hatbox, Elizabeth looked skeptical and

---

[12] *The Tale of Tom Kitten* by Beatrix Potter is a children's story, first published in 1907.

remarked that she had not anticipated adding a hat to the
window display.

"No, not a hat," Betty laughed. "Look, here." She opened
the lid, and what lay inside was not a gentleman's hat.
There was a collection of wooden toys (the kind that
Samuel crafted at the lumberyard); soft cloth toys; and satin
ribbons of every color. The wooden toys included figurines
of animals and boats, similar to what Samuel had made this
year. Among the cloth toys were several ragdolls with hair
of yarn and button eyes. These dolls were Bea's creation.
She had sewn them by hand when Betty was a child, and
Betty could not bear to part with them when she grew
older. So, instead of gifting the dolls to the school, as Bea
had once suggested, Betty decided to put them to use in the
bookshop.

Five years ago or so, she started placing the dolls in the
shopfront window during the holidays. They quickly drew
the attention of children passing by the shop with their
mothers, and Betty found that a lively window display
persuaded more customers to come inside and make a
purchase. Since then, Betty reserved December as the time
to bring out the hatbox, and indeed it was the only time
now that the ragdolls and the other items appeared in the
window. This made the December window unique, and
Betty loved the task of dressing it the first of the month.
Betty also kept additional wooden toys (hand-crafted by
Samuel and Clarence) and dolls (sewn by Bea) in stock in
case the children who visited the bookshop wished to
purchase one. She lined the toys atop the children's section
of the Fiction bookshelf, and could easily use her father's
old footstool to reach them. Last year, in fact, several little
girls had asked to have a doll, and Betty was more than
happy to oblige. She wrapped the dolls in paper tied with a

colorful ribbon, and had watched the little girls bounce out of the shop with their mothers reminding them that the doll was their Christmas gift. Bea's mother was able to stitch numerous dolls at a quick pace, and the children loved them.

She recounted this history to Elizabeth, who was immediately in favor of adding the dolls, toys, and some select ribbons to the window. Thus, it was decided that the shopfront window would be a whimsical and eclectic showcase of children's curios and literature. Winter at The Sapphire Key was largely a season for parents to come into the shop in search of books to keep their children occupied during the holiday, or to give as gifts. The window display would do the trick, and the presence of Leopold would be the cherry on top.

CR

Thomas stopped by towards the end of the day. He had spent the morning and a large part of the afternoon proofreading a manuscript. He had also taken a call from his associate, John, who had resumed travelling and was currently in New York for the T.Y.L. book showcase at a bookstore in Brooklyn. The new associate hire, a young man named Charles Bunton, had a sharp mind and was working out well. He managed the office in Washington while John and Thomas were away, which was good enough for now. Thomas reported that he and John would revisit this arrangement after the holidays.

He did not add to this, though it did make Betty wonder what Thomas' plans were. She thought she might ask him whether, or when, he planned to return to Washington, but not before Christmas.

She would ask him after the New Year, she reasoned.

For now, they were all too busy with other things.

As she tidied the bookshop counter, Thomas stood admiring the window. Leopold had joined him, with a mischievous look in his green eyes as if he was contemplating jumping onto the sill again. He seemed to know that Betty and Thomas would scold him if he did jump, so he merely gazed at the toys in the window longingly as he swished his tail back and forth.

"May I say, another job well-done?" Thomas complimented, as he leaned forward to admire the finished window. Betty and Elizabeth had laid out a burgundy-colored tablecloth in the window on which to arrange all of the books and curios. The Beatrix Potter books were propped up on bookstands, and surrounded by a cluster of wooden toys and several ragdolls. Betty had tied a burgundy ribbon in the dolls' yarn hair, and also tied a ribbon into a bow around one of the books. It was quite festive and would surely delight the holiday shoppers.

"Is this Mr. Samuel Clarkson's work that I detect?" Thomas added.

Betty smiled and walked over to join him. "I assume that you're referring to the wooden toys," she replied, to which Thomas nodded, and she continued. "Yes, that is his work. You see now that his craftmanship is popular all over town. I'm impressed that you recognize it."

Thomas grinned. "I *have* been at the lumberyard to see his work more than once, remember?"

Betty uttered a soft laugh. "Yes, and that reminds me that I have yet to see *your* work!"

Thomas' eyes twinkled, and he said, "All in good time."

Betty frowned slightly at being put off, though secretly enjoyed the anticipation of waiting to see what Thomas had created. "I'll hold you to that," she warned teasingly, and he simply smiled in response before changing the subject to their plans for the evening. He had asked if Betty wanted to join him at the nearby bakery, where Mrs. Highley had placed an order for gooseberry pie. While she baked her own desserts most of the time, this pie was the one dessert that she ordered from the bakery, and Thomas had offered to pick it up for her. Betty agreed to accompany him, and planned to order them cups of hot chocolate while they were there. The baker's hot chocolate recipe rivalled that of any other café or coffee shop, and Betty had always wished for the recipe. She could imagine serving it in her own coffee shop one day.

"Are you about ready?" Thomas asked.

"I am," she replied. "I'll just get my coat." She quickly walked to the back end of the shop towards the storage room to gather her belongings. As she took her coat from the coatrack, she turned her head. Out of the corner of her eye, she saw Thomas toss an envelope into the trash can. Thomas smiled at her once she walked back to the front of the shop, and asked, "Ready to go?"

Betty nodded, gave the shop a final look-over before turning the key into the lock, and then they were on their way.

"The shop window really does look fantastic," Thomas remarked.

"Thank you," Betty murmured. "I enjoy dressing it up for the holidays. Though, it's hard to believe that we're in December already."

"I know," he replied. "And I wonder if it will pass by as quickly as November did."

Betty smiled. November had passed quickly for her as well, with the highlight being the recent Thanksgiving holiday. Thinking on that for a moment, she asked, "Did you enjoy Thanksgiving?"

"I did. The Highleys are good, generous people."

Betty nodded, acknowledging the truth of that conclusion.

"It's made me more curious about Mrs. Highley's sister, Sarah. She told me that they have always been close."

"That's what I know as well," Betty responded. "By the way, did Mrs. Highley give you her sister's address?"

Thomas patted the pocket of his vest. "Yes, I have it. I wondered, actually, if we might talk about the letter soon."

"Oh, certainly," Betty replied. She was pleased that he had the address, and that the plan to write the letter was now in motion.

"Thank you."

Betty was happy to help, though was certain that Thomas would be able to find the words easily once he put pen to paper. Still, she appreciated being part of it. They were in this together, and Betty would not want it to be any other way.

They approached the door of the bakery, and were greeted by the lingering scent of bread that had been baked earlier in the day. Thomas announced that he was picking up an order for Mrs. Highley, and the baker responded, "Ah, yes, I've been expecting you. And, hello, Ms. Featherwin. A hot chocolate for you?"

Betty had frequented the bakery enough times (as had everyone in Marshfield) that the baker was familiar with her favorite order. "Yes, please," she responded. "And make it two."

Betty and Thomas sat down at a table, and soon the baker delivered to them a box containing the gooseberry pie, and two cups of steaming hot chocolate. Thomas looked at Betty inquisitively as the cups were placed on their table.

"Just try it," she encouraged. "I promise, you won't be disappointed."

Thomas complied, bringing the cup to his lips, and Betty in turn took a sip from her own cup. The chocolate was just sweet enough, with a hint of cinnamon and another spice that Betty could not quite detect, and the result was delicious.

"Well, you're right," Thomas said, after taking another sip. "That is quite good. I hope to see this in your own coffee shop one day."

Betty's eyes widened as he said this. Did he know that she had been thinking the exact same thing, for years now? She simply smiled, and enjoyed the moment for a few seconds longer, before she said, "We'll see. Now, you said that you have Sarah Mitchell's address?"

"Yes, and I wanted to show you..." He took a moment to draw a card from his vest pocket. "Her full name is Sarah Mitchell Mount," he explained, showing the card to her. On it, in Mrs. Highley's slanted handwriting, was the name *Sarah Mitchell Mount*, as Thomas had indicated, and below that were the lines of an address. The location was Gate, Oklahoma. "She married a man named Mount, and has eight children, including May Mount, who Mrs. Highley said you met."

"Yes, indeed," Betty responded, looking down at the card, and recollecting that Mrs. Highley's extended family did originate from the southern states—Missouri, Oklahoma, Kansas—as did her Featherwin relatives. "I met May Mount—well, May Mount-Mosier—and her daughter, Florence, earlier this year when they came for a visit. Actually, that was the day when we all had tea and talked about your parents—though we didn't realize who they were at the time."

"Funny," Thomas remarked, and Betty nodded in agreement.

"So, we know now that she lives in Oklahoma. I wonder if that's where your mother also lived, or if she was just visiting Sarah?"

Thomas shook his head, likely wondering the same thing, and replied, "There's only one way to find out."

છ

As they were leaving the bakery, Thomas mentioned that he wanted to deliver the pie to Mrs. Highley right away, and then would walk Betty and Leopold home.

Betty thought for a moment, and responded, "Why don't you meet us back at the shop? I need to pick up some papers I left behind."

Thomas agreed and promised to see them soon, and then walked in the opposite direction.

Betty watched him walk away for a moment, the pie in his hands, and then she and Leopold started off towards the bookshop. When they arrived, she unlocked the door and Leopold padded in ahead of her. He gave a vocal meow, as if to announce his presence, and then sat down to wait for Betty as she went to the front counter.

She was quickly able to locate the papers she needed, and proceeded to place them neatly into her shoulder bag. As she did so, her eyes unconsciously drifted towards the trash can. She could see the white envelope that Thomas had tossed there. The back of the envelope was facing up, and it appeared to be perfectly sealed. Betty tried to dismiss it, and began to move from behind the counter. However, before she walked by the trash can entirely, she reached down to pick up the letter. She had the envelope in her hands, and could see that it was addressed to Thomas Erwinshire, in care of the Marshfield Inn. The return address on the upper left-hand corner stated, Violet Erwinshire; Dayton, Washington. Betty could see that the envelope was indeed sealed securely, with no indication that it had ever been opened.

She looked at it for a moment longer. She did not know what to do with it, but she did not want to leave it in the shop or throw it back into the trash can. Without thinking, she slipped it into her coat pocket.

With another glance at the counter, she called Leopold and the two of them waited for Thomas. He arrived in ten minutes' time to accompany them to the Featherwin house. Along the way, they engaged in idle chatter. Thomas recounted that Mrs. Highley was very pleased about the pie and could not wait to serve it. The walk was swift, and they soon arrived. As Thomas saw them to the front porch, he thanked Betty for coming with him to the bakery.

"I appreciated the company, and the delicious hot chocolate," Thomas said.

Betty smiled in response. "I was happy to join you. Thank you for walking us home."

Thomas dipped his head, and knelt down to pat Leopold. "I'll say goodnight, then, and I'll see you soon."

"Good night," Betty responded, waving as Thomas headed down the street back to the Highleys.

She turned to close and lock the door, and was greeted by her mother, Bea.

"You've made it home in time for dinner," Bea exclaimed happily. "Put down your things and come join me in the kitchen," she urged. "Leopold can come in and eat too."

Betty grinned, returning her mother's embrace. "Let me set this in my room," she responded, gesturing to her shoulder bag. "Then I'll join you." She paused and picked up on the scent wafting from the kitchen. "It smells so good."

"Bean and vegetable soup," Bea remarked. "Hurry before it gets cold."

Betty assured her that she would, and headed down the hallway with Leopold following after her. When she arrived in her room, she put her shoulder bag down and then started to unfasten the buttons of her coat. As her fingers moved to each button, she felt the sharp corner of the envelope. She glanced down, and saw it sticking out of her pocket. For a moment, she had forgotten that she had taken it with her.

She pulled it out, and felt a slight heat rise in her cheeks. It felt somehow wrong to take it out of the trash, and she started to wonder why she did it.

"What do I do with this?" she wondered aloud, and Leopold responded with a meow. She looked up to see the cat's bright green eyes staring at her. She had not been expecting him to answer her, and it startled her a little. Knowing that Bea was waiting for her, she simply slipped the envelope underneath her pillow and put it out of her mind.

◌౩

They enjoyed the pleasant dinner of hot soup, and Leopold was content with a plate of fish. After cleaning their bowls, Bea remarked that she was feeling tired after the long day and told Betty that she was going to turn in early. Betty agreed with this plan, and thought it would be good for her to call it an early night as well. Bea wished her a good night's sleep, stroked Leopold on the head, and headed towards her room. Betty turned down the lamps for her and then followed suit. It had been a long and busy day, and it would certainly not hurt to get some extra sleep, she thought.

She changed into her nightclothes, propped open the window a smidge for Leopold, and then pulled back the covers and slid into bed. As she did so, she noticed that something fell to the floor. She quickly realized it was the envelope she had pulled out of the trash can at the bookshop. She reached down to retrieve it and felt her face flush again.

She did not know what caused her to do it, but curiosity got the best of her. Without fully thinking about it, she opened the envelope and unfolded the letter inside. What was written on it would cause her to have a restless night. Before she could stop herself, her eyes scanned the first line of the letter, and then the next. She sunk down onto her bed and began to read it.

⍥

When Betty awoke the following morning, she had a slight headache. She did not sleep well. She went over the contents of the letter in her head and, line for line, ran through it again. She knew that the letter could be devastating to Thomas and must always remain a secret.

After making this promise to herself, she got up and began her day. As she made her way to work, she was not sure how she would get through the day.

Chapter 10

Snowfall

The second week of December marked the first snowfall of the season in Coos County. The residents all awoke to a thin layer of frost on the windows and a blanketing of white upon the streets and rooftops. The snow was light, at just several inches deep, though this was enough to excite the young children in Marshfield who were eager to play outdoors.

The snow also proved to be a novelty for Leopold. On Friday afternoon, as Betty walked through town, the cat trod delicately alongside her and left behind large pawprints with each careful step he took. Betty smiled as she watched him hop over a water puddle that had frozen over.

"Leopold, haven't you seen snow before?" she murmured fondly.

He looked up at her and twitched his whiskers, an expression on his furred face that seemed both bemused and intrigued.

"Hello there, you two."

Betty turned around at hearing a male voice behind her, and was pleased to see James Smithson. James was Edith's brother. He worked as a millwright at the lumberyard. He had been busy with his work lately, and with helping out in his mother's giftshop, so it had been some time since Betty had seen him.

"James," Betty greeted, and paused in her steps to allow him to catch up to her. "This is a nice surprise."

Leopold meowed pleasantly and weaved around James as he approached.

James was of strong build, and had the bone structure and coloring that acknowledged his Coos Indian heritage. His mother's family all descended from the Coos tribes, and still honored their stories and traditions. James was more traditional than Edith, in many respects, and had been the one to tell Betty much of what she knew about the native history of the town. He had also been the one to give Betty the idea that Leopold was an extraordinary cat. He often said that animals and plants have their own spirits, their own identities, and names of their own choosing, and that cats especially had unique abilities. Although this was, admittedly, Coos myth, Betty tended to believe in it after meeting Leopold.

James remembered Leopold straight away, and said, "Nice to see you again, Leopold. I see that you're reacquainting with the snow."

The cat dipped his head as if he were nodding—or maybe he was simply shaking off a snowflake that had fallen onto his nose.

"I'm not sure he likes it," Betty remarked with a smile.

"Perhaps not. And, it's nice to see you too."

"Yes, we missed seeing you over Thanksgiving," Betty responded. "Did you and your mother join the Clarksons for the holiday?"

"We stopped by the day after Thanksgiving," James answered, kneeling for a moment to pet Leopold. "We spent Thanksgiving day with mother's family."

James and Edith's mother, Ruth Smithson, had extended family who lived a bit further south in the Coquille region of Oregon. As Betty recollected, the Smithson family was heavily involved in the fishery. The estuary in Coquille was rich in salmon, and much of Marshfield's supply came from that region.

"That sounds like a nice day," Betty commented.

"It was," James acknowledged. "It was good to catch up. Everyone is doing well."

"I'm glad to hear it."

"And Samuel and Edith looked well. He is making her happy, I think."

Betty nodded. James cared about his sister's happiness and had been pleased when she and Samuel married. Samuel and James were longtime friends. "Yes, I think so too," she replied. "Have you seen the wooden toys Samuel has made?"

"Yes, I have. He actually stopped by mother's shop last week with a delivery of toy boats. He told me that he had been making wooden toys again, and that Clarence and Thomas had joined him."

Betty nodded. "Yes, they did."

"I'm sorry to have missed the fun. I often work in a different part of the lumberyard than Samuel and Clarence, so I haven't seen much of them."

"That's a shame. Yes, they all spent some time working on wooden toys. Thomas told me that he has enjoyed woodworking, though I've yet to see what he has created."

"There may be a few surprises underway at the lumberyard—but you didn't hear it from me," James answered with a wink.

Betty raised her eyebrows, and was tempted to press James about it, but decided to let the comment pass.

"So, what brings you into town?" she asked as they resumed walking.

James smiled and answered, "The Marshfield winter festival, of course." He referred to the schedule of events that was held in the town square every year on the second

Saturday of December. This year, the event would be held on Saturday, the eleventh of December. The event—which included hayrides, sledding, and rounds of hot chocolate—was Marshfield's celebration of the winter season. It was not quite as grand as a typical festival in Coos County would otherwise be, but was certainly just as lively. Those who lived and worked in North Bend, like James, always came into town for the festivities.

"I know I'm a day early," James continued. "I had an errand to run for mother, and it was a happy circumstance bumping into you and Leopold. I'm planning to come back tomorrow with mother for the festival. Samuel and Edith should be coming by too."

Betty smiled. "Wonderful. It should be a fun time, with the snow on the ground."

James nodded, then glanced down at his watch. "Oh, it's time that I leave you; I must get back to the mill." He returned his gaze to Betty and said, "I'll see you tomorrow in the town square."

"Yes, you will," she replied. He took her hand briefly in parting, and then, with a wave to Leopold, started heading

down the main street towards the row of parked Model-T cars and climbing into one.

"Well," Betty murmured to Leopold, as they resumed their walk back to the bookshop, "Are you going to stay inside tomorrow, or will you insist on coming to the festival too?"

Leopold responded with a vocal meow, and Betty easily understood what he meant.

℘

The following day found Betty, Bea, and Thomas walking into town for the winter festivities, with Leopold accompanying them, of course. The Highleys and the Sattons (who lived in close proximity to the Featherwins) had joined them as well, so they made a large walking party. All were in good spirits. The festival was mainly meant to entertain the children who were out of school, but, in truth, the adults enjoyed it just as much. There was plenty to do, and many people to talk to, and the environment overall was festive.

Thomas had caught up to Betty as their group walked down the street. "Good morning, Betty," he greeted pleasantly.

"Good morning to you," she responded, smiling broadly. He looked well, and his mood was lighter, as though a small weight had been lifted from his shoulders. In truth, it had. After their chat in the bakery, they had discussed the letter to Sarah Mitchell Mount and shared ideas about how to write it. Then, later that week, she and Thomas sat down in the Reading Room to look over a draft Thomas had prepared. Betty offered a few minor suggestions, but otherwise felt that Thomas' version was well-done.

In the letter, Thomas had introduced himself, including his family history and how he had come to know Mrs. Alice Highley. He described the photographs he had of his mother, May Bell Sebastian, and his wish to learn more about her. He ended by asking if Sarah remembered his mother, and if so, whether she would be willing to share memories of her. He closed the letter with an expression of thanks, and a way to reach him, and then signed his name.

The letter now was enclosed in a postmarked envelope and on its way to Sarah. With the delays of the post, doubled now because of the holidays, it was unclear when the envelope would reach its destination. Betty and Thomas hoped it would arrive to Sarah soon, as they were increasingly eager to know what her response to it would be.

Betty could visibly detect Thomas' relief upon sending the letter, and that relief and lightheartedness was still with him now. He was in bright spirits about the festival, as she could tell, and even Leopold had a bounce in his step. The cat had come to good terms with the snow and treaded through it confidently. It made Betty want to laugh.

"Leopold looks to be in fine spirits," Thomas remarked, as he too noticed the cat's confident air.

Betty *did* laugh then. "As we *all* are today, it seems." She looked at Thomas with a smile. "I'm glad you're joining us."

"Me too. I'm told that this is an annual event."

"It is," Betty nodded. "It's a small affair compared with the town's other events, though arguably is the highlight of the season."

"I can see why," Thomas responded. They had come upon the town square now, and it was clear that festivities were already in place. There was a thin layer of snow on the ground, and light flurries swirled in the sky. A good number of people were gathered, chatting together. Many had cups of hot chocolate in their hands, and others were standing together and humming a holiday tune around a man who was sitting on a large bale of hay playing the guitar. Children were laughing and playing in the gazebo in the center of the square, their parents warning them not to run on the snow and ice.

The baker had set up a booth to offer the cups[13] of hot chocolate and individual pastries to the festival attendees. He was doing very well so far—his booth was currently surrounded by folks wanting to purchase the treats.

On the other side of the square were two large wagons filled with bundles of hay for seating. On the side of each wagon was a painted sign that read, "All Aboard for a Hayride." One wagon was hitched up to two horses, and the other was pulled by two good-sized mules. The horses and mules waited patiently, occasionally tossing their heads and stomping their front hooves on the ground. They had been groomed and prepped for driving the wagons: they wore harnesses and around their necks was a garland necklace. As the wagons made their way around the square, the passengers would often sing Christmas carols. It was picture perfect for this happy holiday event.

---

[13] See footnote 5 on the disposable "dixie cup."

There was also a small area where someone had carefully built a campfire and was showing some children how to roast marshmallows. A short distance from the campfire, there was a table where school children could make crafts. Some were pulling yarn through empty spools of thread, to be used as a garland to drape around a Christmas tree. Other children were making tree ornaments.

Then, along the small, snow-covered hill, another group of children were gathered around several wooden sleds. It appeared, from what Betty could see from a short distance, that Samuel Clarkson was standing in the middle of the group, demonstrating to the children how to safely use the sleds. Betty looked on in astonishment, and then caught Thomas' sparkling eye.

"Is that the surprise that Samuel was working on?" she asked.

Thomas smiled and nodded. "Yes, and I may have helped him."

"Oh!" Betty exclaimed. "Now, that *is* a nice surprise." She looked over the throng of people to obtain a better glimpse of the sleds, and as she did so, Elizabeth caught up to them. She had just left her mother, Margaret; Betty's mother, Bea; and the Highleys near the gazebo, where folding chairs had been set underneath a canopy.

"Are you going to watch the sledding?" she asked, placing her hand on Betty's shoulder to announce her presence.

"Yes," Betty replied, turning towards her. "Thomas?"

"You and Elizabeth go on ahead," he suggested. "Leopold and I will catch up to you in a moment."

He assured Betty with a nod when she gave him an inquiring look, and then she went ahead with Elizabeth through the crowd towards Samuel and the sledders. They reached a jovial group of children, ranging from age seven through age fourteen, all eager to take a turn on a sled. There were five sleds crafted from wood. The design of each was sturdy, and it was clear that Samuel and Thomas had taken the time to shape and smooth the wood and to round the rear runners for safety. In addition, unlike the sleds commonly in production, these sleds had a backing for support and to help prevent the sledder from flying forward and incurring injury.[14]

Samuel gave a quick wave to Betty and Elizabeth, and then gestured behind him. Glancing in that direction, they saw Edith sitting on a bench. They quickly walked over to join her.

"Hello, ladies," she greeted, standing to embrace them both.

"Edith, I had no idea that Samuel was so skilled at building sleds," Betty remarked.

"Nor did I," Edith responded, somewhat dreamily, and added, "My Samuel never ceases to surprise me."

"I didn't know Thomas was so skilled either," Elizabeth murmured. She had overheard Thomas admit to helping Samuel.

"I suppose that's the project he's been working on," Betty offered.

"No, actually—" Edith began to say, then stopped herself mid-sentence.

Betty eyes narrowed curiously. "What were you saying, Edith?"

Edith just gave her a coy look and did not answer. Lucky

---

[14] The "flexible flyer" was the sled in production in 1920. Its early version did not have safety features such as rounded runners or a backing.

for her, she was saved from doing so by the return of Thomas.

"Ladies," he greeted, and approached them with a cup in each hand. "A hot chocolate for you," he said, handing one cup to Elizabeth, "And one for you," he continued, handing the other to Betty with a soft smile.

Betty felt warm as her hands wrapped around the cup. "Thank you," she murmured, meeting his eyes with her own. "Didn't you get yourself one?"

"I'm afraid the line was growing long, and I wanted to get back. I'm sorry I didn't get one for you, Edith."

"Oh, Samuel has done that already, Mr. Erwinshire, but thank you anyway," she replied, pointing to the empty paper dixie cup beside her. "Please, sit down and join me to watch the sledders."

They agreed, and the four of them (plus Leopold, curled at Betty's feet) sat upon the bench to watch as the children began taking turns sledding down the hill. Samuel was doing a fine job guiding them. This was not too surprising, as Samuel's job at the mill included overseeing a team of machinists, which was arguably a more challenging endeavor.

"You should take more credit for your work," Betty muttered to Thomas as she slowly slipped her beverage.

"The sleds? The hard labor was all Samuel—I truly only stepped in to sand and polish."

"I meant your other project," Betty rejoined, turning to look at him with a raised eyebrow.

"I don't know what you mean," Thomas replied, though his tone of voice and expression hinted otherwise.

Betty just shook her head, earning a soft, subtle laugh from Thomas. She was determined to find out what other project he had been working on, and why it was such a secret. She strove to refocus her attention on the sledders and let the subject rest for now, but planned to find an opportunity later on. Clearly, Edith knew something about Thomas' project. The secrecy was all very irksome and intriguing.

"In a bit, do you all want to take a hayride?" Thomas asked, effectively changing the subject.

"That sounds like great fun," Elizabeth commented. Edith and Betty agreed. They planned to wait for Samuel to finish supervising the sledders, and then all go on a ride. In just a quarter of an hour, they were ready, and made their way to the other side of the square towards the wagons.

They were directed to a wagon led by two, beautiful jet-black horses with braided manes. The caretaker at the horse barn did an exceptional job with these horses, and it showed. Their coats were soft and their hooves shined. Horses were beloved in Coos County, and respected, and many horse owners doted on their animals as if they were their own children. Even Old Joe, the workhorse at the shipyard, had been loved by all, and a memorial service had been held for him when he passed after over a decade of service in 1903.[15]

The five of them plus Leopold easily fit into one wagon, so they were able to ride together. Inside of the wagon were bundles of hay to be used as benches, covered with folded blankets. After they all took a seat, Leopold jumped into Betty's lap for the ride.

The conductor, who steered the wagon and guided the horses, sat in the front on a slightly elevated podium. "Everybody in?" he called.

---

[15] "Old Joe" was indeed a workhorse for the Coos Bay shipyards. See *North Bend* by Dick and Judy Wagner, cited above in footnote 5.

After they all answered him, he took hold of the horses' reins and encouraged them forward. The horses moved at a slow trot to allow them a leisurely trip around the perimeter of the square. The light snowfall had ceased, though the air remained brisk and felt invigorating on their faces. From her seat in the wagon, nestled in between Edith and Elizabeth, Betty had a nice view of the entire square. The children were at play—some in the gazebo, some on benches, and some sitting in a circle on the ground. Betty could see that many of the younger children had wooden toys in their hands and were making up a game with them. These must have been the toys that Clarence had dropped off to the school. She realized then that she had not seen him since they had first arrived and he disappeared into the crowd. She allowed her gaze to drift in an attempt to find him, though with so many people and things to look at, it was an impossible task. They would seek him out after the hayride.

Continuing on around the square, she saw a few people clustered together with guitars who had started playing music for the people seated in the folding chairs near the gazebo. Betty saw her mother, and Elizabeth's mother, among the people sitting to enjoy the performance. The baker's booth had a sign upon it on which the words, "Be Back Soon!" were printed in large letters. She smiled, and remarked that the baker clearly needed to replenish his supply. The bakery did well throughout the year, and Betty would not be shocked to learn that profits increased during this winter season. The desserts and hot chocolate were such popular items in December.

As they rounded the curve, another horse drawn wagon travelled just ahead of them. It pulled four passengers. From the slight distance, and with the passengers' backs to them, she could not detect who they might be.

"Oh, there's James and Mr. Highley in that wagon," Edith suddenly remarked. She had leaned forward to have a better look. Betty followed her gaze and realized that Edith was correct. James Smithson, Edith's brother, sat across from Clarence Highley. They were joined on either side by Mrs. Alice Highley and a young woman who Betty did not recognize.

"Let's catch up to them when they've finished their ride," Edith suggested. They all agreed.

Betty nudged Edith and asked, "Do you know who that woman is riding with them?"

Edith shook her head. "I can't tell from here. She could be someone James knows."

"I wonder if she's an out-of-towner," Betty mused, and Edith shrugged in a disinterested sort of way.

Thomas and Samuel had been chatting amongst themselves during the ride, largely about baseball and how Samuel was looking forward to getting back on the field when the snow cleared up.

"You'd be great on the local team," Samuel was saying. "You have a natural swing."

Thomas laughed. "We shall see. I do enjoy the game—I'll grant you that."

Betty smirked. Skilled at woodworking *and* at baseball? There was still much to find out about Mr. Thomas Erwinshire.

In a few minutes, they came to a stop, with the horses shaking their heads and giving a soft neigh to announce their return to the starting point.

"All right, folks. Watch your step as you get out of the wagon, and enjoy the rest of the festival," the conductor instructed.

Samuel and Thomas stepped down from the wagon first, and then helped Betty, Elizabeth, and Edith down. Leopold hopped out without any assistance.

"I enjoyed that. Did you?" Betty asked as she took Thomas' offered hand to assist her in stepping down. There was some ice on the ground, so he kept his hand at her back to ensure that she did not slip. Samuel did the same for Edith and Elizabeth.

"I did," he responded. "It's a fine day so far."

Betty agreed. They gathered off to the side to wait for James' wagon to return, and when it did, they came forward to greet them.

"There you are, brother," Edith said as she reached to take his hand. "I was looking forward to seeing you, and then you went off in another wagon," she continued.

"Only because yours was already occupied," he rejoined, and then turned to say hello to the rest of their party. Clarence and his mother exchanged hello's as well, and then the young woman who had been riding with them stepped forward next to Clarence.

She was a stranger to them, though there was something familiar in her face that Betty could not quite place. She had a clear complexion and bright eyes, and the dark hair underneath her hat was styled in a bun, with a few strands loose to frame her face. Her long, navy-blue winter coat, trimmed in fur at the sleeves and collar, and the leather gloves on her hands, were suggestive of the society she ran in.

"I'd like to introduce Ms. Inez Delzell. She is visiting from out of town," Clarence said. The woman gave a small smile and nodded as Clarence made the rounds of introducing everyone to her. His mother replied, "We're delighted to meet you," and Edith (who was always eager to learn about new acquaintances as quickly as possible) rushed forward to engage the woman in conversation.

As the Highleys and the Clarksons were engaged in speaking with Ms. Delzell, the rest of them (James, Thomas, Betty, Elizabeth, and Leopold) went their own way. Elizabeth decided to join her mother and Bea in listening to music. Leopold found a group of children who had been yearning to pet and play with him. Meanwhile, James, Thomas, and Betty sought out James' mother, Ruth, and found her near the baker's booth.

The baker had just returned with another supply of pastries, hot chocolate, and serving cups, so their timing was perfect. Betty quickly purchased a drink and pastry for Thomas (as he had been deprived of the treats earlier) and then ordered another drink for herself, and one for Ruth. James declined.

Ruth spent a few moments updating them on her giftshop (she had woven some baskets which she just put up for sale, and Samuel had delivered his wooden toys) and then they began discussing their respective plans for Christmas. Ruth was looking forward to having her son *and* daughter with her and their extended family in Coquille for the holiday. Edith and Samuel would spend Christmas day with Ruth's family, and the day after with the Clarksons. It was a good compromise.

The Featherwin-Highley family affair would take place at the Featherwin house, Betty explained. Bea was already beginning to decorate the house, including putting a pine tree in the front parlor.

Betty also updated Ruth and James that she had decorated the bookshop windowfront, and they promised to stop by and take a look before returning to North Bend.

The hours passed by quicker than expected, and before long, the sky was beginning to grow dark. This signaled the end of the festival, and time for everyone to rejoin their families. Fortunately, Betty did not need to search for Leopold. Just as she was beginning to wonder where he was, he appeared at her feet, meowing cheerfully and looking as though he had enjoyed the day too.

"Hello there, cat. Glad you found us," said Thomas to Leopold. "Shall we find your mother and the Highleys?" he asked Betty, turning to her.

"Yes, let's," she replied. "I think they're all over by the gazebo."

"We'll walk over that way with you," James offered, indicating that his parked car was on that side of the street.

As they walked the short distance, Betty asked James, "Did you know Ms. Delzell?" She was still curious about the woman, and wondering why Clarence had not mentioned her before, as he seemed to know her.

"I didn't before today," James responded. "But I have a feeling we'll learn more about her soon enough. What do you think, Thomas?"

Thomas, who walked at Betty's other side, shrugged and replied, "I can only say that Clarence looked taken with her."

Betty pursed her lips and wondered at the implication of their statements before they reached their destination and came together with Bea and the Highleys.

There was a change in the tides this winter season. The snowfall resumed as they all started back home, and Betty wondered how things might develop between Christmas and the new year.

Chapter 11

Christmas

"That's beautiful," Betty remarked. She was watching her mother, Bea, put the finishing touches on their pine tree in the parlor. The tree was about six feet in height. Bea had set it upon a circular rug near the fireplace and had spent the last week or so gradually adding decorations to it. She had done a fine job, and the tree looked marvelously festive. It was bedecked in ruby-red ornaments, with garlands of popcorn and cranberries. Red ribbons were tied in a bow on the branches to hang each ornament, and additional crimson-colored bows filled the remaining spaces on the tree. The fireplace mantel housed some extra decorations originally intended for the tree: small seashell ornaments, several pine cones covered in a gold lacquer, and a large ornament of a red bird. It was truly a joyful display.

Leopold was largely dismissive of the tree, to Bea's surprise. She had expected him to try to knock the tree over and play with the decorations, as cats were inclined to do. However, he was quite well-behaved and paid little attention to Bea's decorating. The only thing that eventually caught Leopold's eye was the red bird on the mantle.

As soon as Betty took the ornament out of its box and arranged it next to the gold pine cones, Leopold was at her feet in a flash. He had meowed at Betty in a pitiful way, and began swishing his tail as he stared at the bird. Betty merely laughed and stroked his head, saying, "It's not a *real* bird, you know." Leopold seemed to think otherwise, and continued to stare at it longingly. He had, thus far, restrained himself from leaping onto the mantel to capture the bird ornament, but now was in the habit of eyeing it in a threatening way every time he passed by the parlor.

As Bea and Betty finished their decorating, Leopold again appeared. This time, he rolled over onto his back, his four feet in the air, as he looked at the red bird.

"Look, mother," Betty laughed. "If only I had a camera, I would take his picture."

Bea joined her in laughing, and replied, "You'll have to capture the moment in your mind for now. Tell me, dear, what do you think?"

Betty took another look at Leopold before he rolled over onto his belly, and then considered the Christmas tree. "Everything about it is perfect," she replied.

Bea, who stood looking at the tree also, said, "I think so, too. The house is beginning to feel like Christmas."

The days since the winter festival had flown by, and their holiday gathering was just two days away. Betty had kept busy at the bookshop with customers still requesting copies of *On the Level* by T.Y.L. Betty had also sold a good number of copies of Beatrix Potter's storybook, and some of Bea's ragdolls, due to the window display. As anticipated, it had attracted parents and their young children. James and his mother, Ruth, had indeed come by the bookshop to take a look at the shopfront window and found it quite charming. James jested that the only thing missing was a tree made out of books. Elizabeth overheard this comment, and surprised Betty the following day with exactly that: she had arranged books into the shape of a tree, near the front counter. This gave them both a good laugh.

Betty had spent her remaining time helping Bea prepare for their holiday guests, the Highleys and Thomas. Bea felt that it was important to put forth a big effort during the holidays, even if her guests had been over to the house countless times and for numerous holidays. This actually made it more imperative to put forth a big effort to decorate the house, and to prepare a meal that would top the previous year's meal. As Bea had always put it, Christmas at the Featherwin house was like Thanksgiving with a little extra magic. When Betty was a child, she thought that Bea referred to real magic, and perhaps she did. The household did feel magical every December, and the feeling was especially potent this year. Betty was not sure why—perhaps it was because Leopold was with them, or perhaps it was because she had been thinking about her father, Henry—but, in any case, this year was a little different and a little more magical. It made her look forward to Christmas dinner even more.

Thomas, meanwhile, continued to reside in the Highley's upstairs guestroom and assisted them as a way of repaying their generosity. Mrs. Highley had insisted that there was no need for Thomas to clean up the kitchen, or to help Mr. Highley tend to the backyard. She was happy to have him as their guest. Still, helping the family was just in Thomas' nature and he continued on with these tasks. In private to Betty, he had confided that he felt like he was overstaying his welcome. Betty told him that assuredly, this was not the case, because Mrs. Highley was a straightforward person and would have told him if he was no longer welcome. This seemed to assuage Thomas' concern momentarily, and he dropped the subject. The truth was, however, that Betty did not know whether Mrs. Highley would be that straightforward with Thomas. Betty likewise did not know if Thomas was planning to leave Marshfield, even if he was still welcome to stay with the Highleys. The question over Thomas' long-term plans had stuck in the back of her mind, and reared its head again. She had planned to ask him about it after the New Year, but what if he made up his mind before then? The notion gave her an uncomfortable feeling.

"Betty, help me decide on a tablecloth," Bea called from the pantry, interrupting Betty's thoughts about Thomas' impending departure.

With a sigh as she cleared her head, she answered, "I'm coming," and walked down the hall with Leopold bouncing along after her.

❧

Christmas day dawned bright and chilly. There had been no more snow since that initial snowfall on the day of the festival, but the days had been brisk and wintry with occasional sprinklings of rain. The evenings were cold enough to leave patches of ice on the windows and on the roads. The air was so cold at night, in fact, that Betty had to close her bedroom window. This perturbed Leopold a little, as he was so used to being free to roam. Once Bea and Betty started decorating, however, he realized how entertaining it was to stay inside rather than go outside. Thus, after just one night of complaining to Betty, he stopped and instead savored curling up by the fireplace and scheming about how to capture the red bird ornament without Betty noticing.

Betty had grown increasingly skilled at reading the cat's moods, and had the feeling that Leopold could detect her moods as well. That would help to explain why, for instance, he had appeared at her side just as she was thinking about him. It would also explain why he curled up right next to Bea one night when she had been thinking about Henry and feeling blue. Bea told Betty the following morning that Leopold had comforted her at just the right moment, as if he

 knew she was feeling sad and needed that comfort. The occurrence that Betty still could not quite explain, however, was how Leopold had known about the impending fire at the Marshfield Inn. Cats were intuitive, she knew, but Leopold's intuition was uncanny. It created a stronger bond between them, though also made her wonder about his abilities and about those old Coos Indian legends and whether there was any truth to them.

Regardless of their truth, Betty *and* Bea could understand Leopold's mood now. He was trotting through the house with a spring in his step, carrying around a red bird in his mouth. Somehow, when no one was watching, he leapt onto the mantel and grabbed the red bird ornament that Betty had placed there. Betty chased him down the hall and finally was able to get the bird out of his mouth. The ornament was not completely unscathed, but she felt that it was salvageable. Leopold had been having so much fun with the bird, and looked downcast about having to relinquish it.

Betty sighed, looking at the cat, and said, "Well, it *is* Christmas. I wasn't going to give you your present until later in the day, but I think now is a good time."

She walked over to her bedroom drawer and took out a soft, cloth red bird that she had been sewing over the last few days. She had stuffed it with some old material to make it look fluffy. Since the first day she saw Leopold staring at the bird ornament on the mantel, she decided that Leopold deserved a Christmas gift just like anyone else. The idea came to her to make Leopold a bird that he could actually keep and play with. Betty was initially skeptical that Leopold would appreciate it, as he did not seem like the kind of cat who liked traditional toys. In this case, she was proven wrong.

When she took it over to Leopold, he immediately started rubbing his face against the toy and purring like an engine. He knocked it in the air a few times, and quickly tossed it around the room. After batting it around between his paws, he picked it up in his mouth and headed towards the kitchen. Betty laughed and followed after him, calling out, "Mother, Leopold has something to show you."

Leopold dropped the bird and meowed at Bea as soon as he arrived in the kitchen.

"Oh, what have you got there?" Bea asked.

He meowed again and resumed playing with the bird and purring. As Betty joined them in the kitchen, Bea looked over at her and said, "He seems so happy with his toy."

Betty nodded and laughed as she watched the cat at play. "Happy" was the perfect way to describe the cat's reaction. "Yes," she agreed. "Leopold loves that bird. Who knew that a simple toy bird would make him act like a playful kitten?"

Bea responded with a gentle laugh as she watched Leopold resume batting the bird between his paws. She was in the midst of baking another batch of sugar cookies. She had already made several kinds of pies (pumpkin, cranberry, and pecan) and a chocolate cake with white icing. All of these sweets would be offered for dessert following Christmas dinner.

After watching Leopold play for a few more moments, adoring his bouncy demeanor, Betty turned to Bea and asked, "What do we need to do next for the party?"

"Let's put the icing for the cake in the icebox, if there is room. I'll cover the cookies and leave them here, on the counter, once they're finished baking."

"That sounds fine to me. What else?"

There was a lot to do, of course, but much of the final preparations and setting of the table would be done closer to the time of the Christmas party. They expected the Highleys and Thomas to arrive at five-o-clock for dinner, which would be followed by dessert and gift exchanges.

"I think that's all," Bea answered with a smile, dusting her hands on her apron. "I can handle the cooking. Why don't you enjoy the rest of the morning? Maybe put a record in the phonograph—something jolly?" Bea uttered this last suggestion with a wink.

"Well, all right," Betty replied, and rose from her chair. "A holiday tune would be nice. Come along, Leopold." Leopold chirped in response, picked up the toy bird in his mouth, and zipped across the hall to beat her to the parlor. The phonograph was there on a stand. The lid was propped open, and beside it on the adjacent table were several records. As Betty drew near, she noticed that the record on the top of the small stack was "The Parade of the Tin Soldiers", a lively and popular Christmas composition. Betty picked up the record and placed it on the turntable to play. She smiled as the sounds of the cheerful instrumental began to resonate.[16]

She placed the other records in the storage cabinet underneath the phonograph, and as she did so, something else caught her eye. Propped on the table, she noticed an envelope with the words, *To Betty—Merry Christmas.*

"Oh," she murmured in surprise, and sat down in one of the armchairs to open it.

Leopold followed her and flopped down at her feet, curious about it, too. The handwriting on the envelope was

---

[16] "The Parade of the Tin Soldiers" was composed in 1911 by composer Leon Jessel, and performed in 1912 by John Philip Sousa. Sheet music and recordings for this popular tune were made available for purchase.

her mother's. With a soft smile, she slipped a finger beneath the flap to discover what lay inside.

There were two items: a note (also in Bea's handwriting) and a photograph. The black-and-white photo was slightly yellowed on the edges, though otherwise looked well-preserved. It depicted a young man with a handsome face, attired in the garments common to the early years of that century, standing in front of a building with a faded sign on the door that read, "Marshfield Grocery." There was something very familiar about the man, and something familiar about the building also. As Betty continued to study it, she thought that the man looked very much like her father, Henry, in his younger days. She turned the photograph over, and was pleased to see an inscription: *Henry, at the shop—1901. Marshfield.*

"Oh my goodness," Betty whispered, and Leopold stood on his hind feet to get a closer look at the photo too. After sniffing it for a moment, he looked at Betty and meowed inquiringly. "This is father," she answered him. "I've never seen this picture of him before." Placing the photograph next to her on the table, she eagerly unfolded the note from her mother.

> *Dearest Betty,* it read,
> *This is, of course, your father, about a year after we married. He stands next to the old Marshfield Grocery. On that day, your father wanted his picture taken in front of the store, and I asked him why. He said that he was going to own that store one day, and he would turn it into an emporium for books, coffee, and collectibles. He claimed that it would be the most profitable business on the street. I thought he was mad, naturally, but I humored him and took the picture like he wanted. This store no longer exists, as it was closed down*

shortly after this picture was taken. Can you guess what stands in its place now? If you can't, I'll give you a clue: your father's fanciful ideas have come to fruition.

All my Love, and Merry Christmas

Betty read the note with an expression of puzzlement on her face. After sitting to think for a few moments, the note in her lap, she came to a sudden realization. "No, it can't be!" she whispered to herself, and took another look at the building in the photograph. Of course, it still looked familiar, but could it be what she was thinking? With a broad smile, she took the note and photograph back to the kitchen.

"I see you've found the right record. Perhaps we should play it during the dinner tonight," Bea greeted as she heard Betty's footsteps. She did not look up at Betty, as she was busy setting the sugar cookies onto a plate.

"I found something else too," Betty replied. Bea looked at her then, and gave her a smile that matched Betty's smile.

Betty came forward to give her mother an embrace. "Thank you, this is wonderful."

Bea placed a kiss on Betty's cheek. "You're most welcome."

"Is this really what I think it is—that the old Marshfield Grocery *is* The Sapphire Key?"

Bea laughed at her daughter's enthusiasm and incredulous expression, and remarked, "Yes, it is! Your father had insight into the future, it seems, or least very good intuition."

The Marshfield Grocery had closed down and stood empty until it was purchased by Henry Featherwin, who had turned it into the bookshop that Betty had inherited from him.

"It sure seems that way," Betty answered, still looking at the photograph and shaking her head.

"What I *can* say about your father, for certain, is that he always went after what he wanted without hesitation. And, he knew he wanted to make a success of that store."

Betty smiled, now focusing on her father's youthful, confident face. "How did he *know* that it would be a success? Buying that building must have been a big risk."

"Yes, it was, and I tried to talk him out of it. He had a good future working at the lumbermill—why throw it away? But he was determined."

Betty looked back up at Bea. She felt a tear in her eye, and Bea reached her hand up to brush it away.

"Merry Christmas, dear."

"Merry Christmas, mother."

The magical feeling of Christmas had arrived, and Betty could not wait to see what other gifts the day and evening would bring.

ℜ

In what seemed like no time at all, the five-o-clock hour arrived and the Highleys and Thomas were due at any moment. The table was set with a red tablecloth and dishware; the lamps were lit; and the phonograph hummed with cheerful music. The Featherwin house was warm and festive, with all of the decorations, delicious food, and joyful energy that one could ever hope for on Christmas.

Their gathering would be modest, but it was the quality of the guests that mattered much more than the quantity. Betty and Bea could not imagine sharing the holiday without their dear friends and neighbors, who they loved so well.

Leopold eagerly waited by the door, meowing and pressing his paw against the doorframe.

"I don't see them coming up the street yet," Bea commented, as she looked out of the window.

"No, but Leopold can sense that they're on their way," Betty responded, coming to join Bea and patting Leopold fondly. "Are you looking forward to seeing our guests?" she asked him. He purred loudly in response.

Bea closed the curtain and looked at Betty and Leopold thoughtfully. "I must admit, that cat has grown on me. And you talk to him as if he can understand you. It reminds me of when your father would talk to that stray cat every afternoon for a month."

Betty did not respond, but smiled softly. It was her secret (and maybe it had been her father's secret too) that the cat could understand her, and she could understand the cat.

"Oh, here they come now," Bea continued, and she was right. The Highleys and Thomas could be seen walking up the street towards the house. Betty felt her heart lift in anticipation. It had been a few years since she had looked forward to Christmas dinner this much, and she enjoyed the feeling.

Even from this distance, Betty could tell from her vantage point at the window that they were in high spirits. Clarence and Thomas were walking together, laughing. Mr. and Mrs. Highley walked just behind them, with Mrs. Highley's hand tucked over her husband's arm. They were all dressed very fine.

"I'll open the door," Betty offered, and did so to admit their guests as Bea came to stand beside her. In a moment, an intermingling of voices uttered, "Merry Christmas" as they all gathered on the porch. Exchanges of "hello" and "how lovely you look" were interspersed between the exclamations of holiday wishes, and Bea was soon encouraging everyone to come inside.

Betty and Thomas followed in after the others. In the brief moment that they remained standing out on the porch, Thomas took her hand, dipping his head in his usual way of greeting, and said, "Betty, I wish you the happiest of Christmases."

Betty's breath caught in her throat for a second as she noticed the warmth in Thomas' eyes, their hazel hue changing in the evening light. "I wish the same to you, Thomas."

He smiled, and then they both went inside to join the others and commence the merrymaking of the holiday.

ᘓ

It was a leisurely dinner, with lots of laughter and good conversation, and the music from the phonograph in the background. After dinner in the dining room, Bea brought out her desserts, with everyone commenting on how good everything looked and taking a small sample of each. Even Leopold enjoyed the mealtime, as he was given a lot of attention and allowed to have a tiny sampling of the dinner food (along with his usual fare of salmon).

Afterwards, they all assembled in the parlor, where Mr. Highley helped in lighting the fireplace to fill the room with warmth and light. Meanwhile, Bea brought in more cookies from the kitchen. A soft snowfall had started outside, and they drew the curtains open to take a look from their snug space inside. The red decorations on the Featherwins' tree gleamed in the firelight as the pleasant buzz of their conversations filled the air. It made for a picturesque winter scene.

Before too long, it was time for gift-giving, an annual tradition. The Featherwins and Highleys did not often indulge in presents, but if they did, Christmas was the time for it. Bea had given Betty her gift earlier in the day, of course, and Betty had followed suit. In the afternoon, she had surprised Bea with a knit, pine-green scarf that she had picked up at Ruth Smithson's giftshop in North Bend at around Thanksgiving time. She had been visiting the giftshop, and the second she saw the scarf, she knew that it would be the perfect Christmas gift for her mother. Ruth (who had knitted the scarf herself) wrapped it neatly in colored paper with a ribbon, and Betty had tucked her own card underneath the ribbon. Bea was delighted with the gift.

The others' gifts were similarly thoughtful. In the midst of the exchanges, and as the topic of conversation shifted to news at the lumberyard and shipyard, Thomas tapped Betty on the shoulder.

"I have something to give you," he murmured softly, with a smile that reached his eyes.

She returned the smile. "So do I," she whispered back, and glanced over at the table by the front door, where a rectangular, wrapped package lay.

"Shall we?" he asked. She nodded, and they moved slightly away from the others and nearer to the door. Betty noticed, as Thomas stood, that he held a wrapped box of his own in his hands. "Leopold won't get jealous, will he?" he asked jokingly.

"No, I don't think he will," she answered, and gestured to the cat, who was snoozing on one of the parlor armchairs, his toy red bird tucked between his paws. "He already is quite content with his gift."

"As I can see," Thomas responded with a soft laugh.

Betty turned to pick up the package from the front table and started to hand it to Thomas, but he stopped her.

"Wait—I'd like you to open mine first."

Betty raised an eyebrow, and said, "I'd be glad to. Any particular reason?"

Thomas eyes sparkled. "Yes, and you'll see when you open it."

Sufficiently intrigued, Betty took the gift from Thomas as he handed it to her and began unwrapping it to reveal a large, white box. On the lid of the box was attached a card which read,

> *Ms. Betty Featherwin,*
> *A gift for you, and one that I hope was worth the wait.*
>
> *Yours,*
> *Thomas Erwinshire*

Betty gave him an inquisitive glance after she read the card, then, with increased anticipation, opened the lid of the box. She drew in a breath, and said, "Beautiful." Inside lay two wooden bookends, beautifully crafted from myrtle wood. She carefully took each of the bookends out, her fingers feeling the smoothness of the sanded and polished wood. They were stunning, with gradations of chestnut-brown throughout. As she turned them over in her hands, she noticed that each bookend bore an intricate and detailed engraving of a cat. The cats' frames had been carved into the wood, and then the small details—nose, whiskers, and mouth—had been carved also. Even the cats' eyes had been engraved, though with even greater detail. A stone or marble, jade-green in color, had been embedded into the wood to give the appearance that the cats had green eyes. It was so clever and so skillfully done that Betty was speechless for the moments she spent admiring the bookends. It was Thomas' voice that eventually regained her attention.

"So, what do you think?" he asked. "Was it worth the wait?"

Betty turned her gaze to his, pondering for a moment, and then the realization struck her, and she let out a gasp. "This is the project you were working on at the lumberyard? They're the most beautiful bookends I've ever seen!"

Thomas smiled and nodded. "I know I've been putting you off, but…"

"Oh, it was definitely worth the wait!" Betty exclaimed, interrupting him. "My goodness, Thomas, these are wonderful."

Thomas laughed and, in the dim light of the room, it appeared as if the tips of his ears reddened slightly.

"So, this is what you were spending time on," she continued, looking at the bookends again. "These cat engravings are so intricate, and the eyes…" She paused as she studied the green stones that made up the eyes, and then recalled that, just before Thanksgiving when they were at Simpson Beach, Thomas had put several jade-colored stones in his pocket.

Thomas seemed to know exactly what she was thinking, for he said, "I found these jade stones when we were at the beach that day, before Thanksgiving. I thought they'd be perfect for the eyes."

Betty only nodded, rendered almost speechless again, before another realization came over her. "These cats…," she responded. "They look a lot like Leopold."

Thomas smiled then, with a thoughtful tilt of his head, and said, "Leopold is part of The Sapphire Key, in a way. So, he had to be part of the bookends too."

"Oh gosh, Thomas," Betty breathed in response, shaking her head. She felt like she had so much more to say to him then, but she settled on, "I just love them."

He understood those words, and all of the other words she did not say, and responded, "I'm very glad."

Betty was caught up in the moment, and almost forgot that she had not yet given Thomas *his* gift. She was reminded when Leopold suddenly came trotting over to inspect his likeness on the bookends.

"Oh, please open yours now," Betty said, reaching beside her for the wrapped gift and handing it to Thomas. With a smile, he proceeded to unwrap the present to reveal a book inside. It was titled, *Coos Bay History and Mythology.* The book contained a rich, historical background of the Coos Bay area, its development, and the impact of the Coos Indian tribes on the area and their traditions and related mythology. It was a book that Betty had read to learn about the history of the town. She knew that Thomas appreciated history as much as she did, and hoped he would find it enjoyable and useful.

"This is fantastic," Thomas murmured, as he opened the book to study the title page. "Historical books fascinate me, and I've always wanted to publish one. The closest I've gotten to publishing a historical account—and this is not straight history—is the novel, *On the Level.*" He looked up at Betty with deep appreciation in his gaze. "Thank you."

Betty blushed slightly, and responded, "Of course. I hope you enjoy it."

"I will," he replied. "It will be particularly enjoyable to read as I'm making my plans."

Betty knit her eyebrows and looked at him curiously. "Your plans?"

"Yes," he nodded. "I told you before that I felt I may be overstaying my welcome at the Highleys, regardless of what

Mrs. Highley says."

Betty felt the color start to drain from her face. So, he had already formed a plan. Was his time in Marshfield already coming to an end? It was a notion that Betty could not fully process in the moment; she was not expecting it; she was not ready for it.

He seemed to notice the change in her expression, for his voice softened, and he placed a hand atop hers. "Betty, I've thought a lot about this, and I've had a number of conversations with my associate. I've decided to open up a branch of Erwinshire Publishing here, in Coos Bay."

Betty felt as though her heart had dropped to the floor and then suddenly returned to her chest. "Truly?" she managed to ask.

"Yes," he answered with a smile. "Truly. You can't get rid of me, I'm afraid."

Betty had the impulse to laugh and throw her arms around him at the same time. In that moment, it felt that the world had shifted and realigned to make sense of things that did not make sense before.

She just replied, "I'm so, so happy to hear this, Thomas."

༺

It had been a merry and magical Christmas in more ways than one, with more surprises and possibilities than Betty could have imagined. When she retired to her room late that evening, after she and Bea had bid farewell to their guests with another round of "Merry Christmas," Betty drifted to sleep with Leopold beside her, wondering, with great hope and anticipation, what the new year would bring.

Chapter 12

New Beginnings

The Christmas season passed in just the same manner as it had arrived: in a flurry of activity. Before the year ended, the Marshfield Inn where Thomas had been staying prior to the fire announced that it was ready to receive guests again. The repairs from the small fire were completed, and it was declared safe for the business to continue operating. Thomas decided that it was time to return to his room there. He thanked the Highleys for their kindness in allowing him to stay at their home while the Inn was undergoing the repairs. He was truly overwhelmed by the generosity that had been shown to him by all of the neighbors and friends he had made in Marshfield. Mrs. Highley insisted that Thomas be a regular visitor, and Thomas promised her that he would. He gathered his belongings, including a lunch that Mrs. Highley had made for him, and went on his way to the Marshfield Inn.

For the time being, he would not return to Washington. He told Betty of his plan ahead of time, of course. He felt more comfortable renting a room for a short while, and he did not like to impose on anyone. He also preferred to work from the Inn, as he was beginning to scout out potential locations for the second branch of Erwinshire Publishing. So far, he had only revealed this to Betty, and did not want word to get out to the Highleys or others—not until he felt more confident that his plan would indeed work out. He expressed to Betty a desire to keep it under wraps until he had found a location and set things into motion. At that time, he reasoned, he would announce his long-term plans to everyone. Betty liked this idea, and appreciated Thomas taking her into his confidence about his plans. Out of respect for his wishes, she would keep his plans a secret until he was ready to divulge them.

Knowing what she knew, Betty was not surprised to see Thomas move back to the Inn before the new year. The only person who was astonished at the move was Edith Clarkson, who had been with her family in North Bend through Christmas and the New Year, and thus had not been aware of the events happening in Marshfield. She had been occupied with family matters.

Betty and Elizabeth had met Edith and a couple of her girlfriends from North Bend at the bakery in early January for hot chocolate. The gathering had been Edith's suggestion. It was typical of Edith to want to catch up on gossip, and it made Betty smile. Even if there was truly no gossip in Marshfield, Edith was sure to discover some.

When they met on Saturday afternoon, that is exactly what Edith did. After ordering hot chocolate and chatting about Christmas, Edith asked how Clarence and Thomas were getting along. Betty told her that they got on very well. During the Featherwin-Highley Christmas dinner, they had shared stories about their woodworking at the lumberyard and making of toys and gifts. Betty then told the ladies about the beautiful gift of bookends that Thomas had made her. She had put them on display in The Sapphire Key at the front counter. Elizabeth and Edith's other friends were touched by the thoughtfulness of such a gift, and Edith remarked that she had expected Thomas all along to give Betty a fitting and unique gift. She said that the men had a good time working with wood and making holiday gifts. This caused Betty to ask Edith if she knew about the bookends.

Edith gave her a smile, and replied, "We all have our secrets, and I may have been asked to keep this one."

Betty smiled, shaking her head, though she understood. Still on the subject of Clarence and Thomas, Edith then inquired how Thomas was faring as a guest of the Highleys. This is when Elizabeth told her that Thomas had moved back to the Inn. To everyone else at the table, this was ordinary news. To Edith, this was prime Marshfield gossip.

For some reason, she was stunned that no one had thought to tell her this before, especially her husband, Samuel. He worked at the mill with Clarence and would surely have learned of it from him or the other workers. She was equally stunned that Thomas chose to return to the Inn, given the state of the building after the fire.

Elizabeth commented in reply, "Well, it was always assumed that the guests would return to the Inn and re-occupy their rooms once the repairs were complete."

Betty nodded. This was true, and she knew that Thomas did not want to impose on anyone. He also enjoyed the quiet atmosphere of the Inn while working.

Edith was still baffled, nonetheless, that Thomas did not choose to stay at the nicer hotel in North Bend.

"I'm just surprised," Edith added. "The Inn pales in comparison in terms of accommodations."

Betty replied, "The Inn is not that bad. It's clean and quiet, and in that regard, it has great appeal."

Edith looked at Betty with a slight frown. Everyone knew that Edith loved to talk, so the quiet Inn would not be ideal for her. Betty did love Edith dearly, but there were moments when Edith failed to consider that what was good for her, might not be suited for someone else.

The topic of Thomas' accommodations grew stale rather quickly, and the conversation transitioned to other subjects. They chatted about small things for a little while, including how they had all spent New Year's Eve. Everyone usually celebrated with a glass of wine at the end of the year. It was a time when drinking was frowned upon by some, but for many in Marshfield and the neighboring cities, wine simply involved a technique of working with grapes. It could certainly be enjoyed in the privacy of one's home. Everyone knew that Prohibition would eventually fail, it was just a matter of when.[17] The ladies felt that it was not wise to get too involved in some of the political happenings, though did keep abreast of any news.

Returning the conversation to the holidays, Edith added that she had purchased a large quantity of pale grey material in North Bend just after Christmas and planned to use it to make skirts and blouses.

"It will be nice to wear them when it starts to warm up. I have enough material for everyone." Her eyes lit up and she added, "Why don't we all get together one Sunday afternoon and have a sewing bee[18]?"

Elizabeth looked a bit concerned, and responded, "That sounds fun, but if we all wear pale grey on the same day, it'll look like we belong to a private club, or a choir."

This just tickled Edith and she burst out laughing, which soon caused everyone else to join her in laughing too. She could hardly contain herself at the thought of seeing everyone all in grey on the same day. It conjured quite an image!

When Edith finally calmed down, she replied, "I never

---

[17] Prohibition refers to a time when the sale and consumption of alcoholic beverages was prohibited; hence, the name "prohibition." The Volstead Act, passed by Congress on October 28, 1919, enforced prohibition at the national level. Prohibition ended in 1933.

[18] A sewing bee is a social gathering (usually of women) based around making or mending clothes.

thought of that. I just thought the material was beautiful and fashionable, and so I purchased a lot of it."

"Well," Betty replied, her own laughter subsiding, "We'll just have to think of something to add to it so that the color grey is not so noticeable."

Edith said, "Yes, I think that will be fine," and the other ladies heartily agreed. It was then decided that, on a Sunday, very soon, the young ladies would get together and do some sewing. It would be pleasant, and an occasion to look forward to.

Shortly afterward, with their cups of hot chocolate empty and the afternoon winding down, the ladies parted each other's company and headed out with a promise that they would all meet again soon.

Betty and Elizabeth walked out together to head back in the direction of The Sapphire Key.

"Well, it's a new year with new beginnings," Elizabeth commented during the walk.

"Yes," Betty replied, "Though not everything needs to be new. Some things stay true and remain the same—like friendship and good company."

Elizabeth smiled at this and said, "I couldn't agree more."

All in all, with their pleasant afternoon, Betty anticipated that the month of January 1921 would bring good tidings. She had her dear friends and family, including Thomas, close by, which made her quite content.

Chapter 13

The Letter

Elizabeth and Betty returned to the bookstore and started to remove the Christmas display in the front window before it was time to close. They replaced the Christmas decorations with a variety of books and the newest magazines. As they were straightening up, and placing the decorations back in the box that was in the storage room, they heard the bell rattle on the front door. Betty walked out of the storage room and towards the front door to say hello to whoever was there. It was a young man who had been helping out at the post office. He introduced himself as Ernest, and said that he was sorting mail and saw a letter addressed to The Sapphire Key for Mr. Thomas Erwinshire.

"...so, I thought I would just walk on down and deliver it in person," Ernest explained. He added, "I've never been in a bookstore before, and wanted to take a look. You sure have lots of books here."

Betty smiled, and said, "Yes, we do," and then asked if he spent much time reading.

He replied, "Yes, ma'am, my mother taught me, but we don't have much to read."

Betty thought for a moment, and said, "I want you to take a look, and choose any book you like, as a gift from me. Consider it a late holiday gift, and a thank you for bringing this important letter to me."

Ernest smiled broadly and replied, "That's very generous of you."

"Not at all," Betty responded. "What subjects do you find interesting?"

"Well, I like fishing boats, and the water."

Elizabeth heard them talking and walked over to them. "Hello," she greeted. "Follow me; we have lots of fishing books." They both walked to the nautical section of the store.

After perusing the shelf for a few moments, Ernest pulled out a book, and with a grin on his face, he said, "I like this one."

Elizabeth beamed and said, "Good choice. It's a beautiful book."

As she walked him out, he turned and said, "Thank You" to Betty.

She looked thoughtfully at him and said, "You're welcome. Your first trip to a bookstore should be a good one".

"Yes ma'am," Ernest replied, and was on his way. Betty figured he was fourteen or fifteen years old.

Betty stood staring at the envelope after the young man left. Before Elizabeth returned to the counter, she put it into her pocket.

Elizabeth looked at Betty and asked, "Well, what do you think that letter is about?"

"Perhaps something to do with his business," Betty responded. It was not her place to discuss Thomas' letter, so she acted as if it was none of her concern.

Elizabeth nodded in understanding and added, "I want to tell you, that was very kind what you did—allowing that boy to choose any book in the store. It was one of the kindness gestures I have ever seen."

Betty's heart warmed to hear her say this. "It felt right," she responded softly. "Maybe one day, he will be a regular customer." She took a glance at her watch, and noticing the time, she added, "Let's close up and get our coats." Elizabeth agreed and helped Betty secure the shop for the evening.

"Well, tomorrow is Sunday, and the shop is closed, so I think I will catch up on some reading myself, and of course, take care of a few chores," Elizabeth said as Betty locked the door. Betty smiled in response, and they walked down the street together.

ରୈ

The following morning found Betty and Bea in their Sunday morning routine of getting ready to attend church. They both anticipated a pleasant service, followed by a quiet afternoon at home. After the excitement of the holidays, it was somewhat nice to return to the normal, peaceful way of things. Betty imagined that Thomas felt the same way. He was probably catching up on work now in the quiet atmosphere of the Inn, she thought.

As she and Bea headed out the door, Betty's thoughts turned for a moment to the letter. She had placed it in the drawer of her bedside table for safekeeping. The moment she had returned home last night, she took a closer look at the envelope and noticed the stamp on the front. It was postmarked January 4, 1921, 11 a.m., Gate, Oklahoma. As soon as she saw this, her heart skipped a beat. There was no return address on the envelope, but the postmark was enough for her to suspect that this was the letter she and Thomas had been waiting for: the letter from Sarah Mitchell Mount. Her fingers tingled with the desire to pull back the envelope flap and find out—but then she realized that she could not. She told herself, "Not again!"

She knew that Thomas must be the one to open it. She also knew that this was not like the first letter she had found in the trash. Clearly, Thomas had no interest in *that* letter.

Betty knew that *this* letter, he wanted to read. She planned to give it to Thomas when she saw him, which she hoped would be tomorrow.

It turned out that she need not wait that long. As they entered the church, Betty was pleased to see Thomas himself, taking a seat in one of the pews. Betty smiled to him from across the room. He noticed and walked towards her, his eyes brightening as he extended his hand to say hello.

"Mr. Erwinshire, it's nice to see you here," Bea said with a smile. "Will you sit with us?"

"If you don't mind, I'd be glad to," he responded.

"We don't mind at all," Betty answered, smiling at him. "I'm happy to see you at this Sunday service," she continued, as they found their way to their seats.

"Being new in town, I thought I should attend one of the services. I may make this part of my normal routine," he answered, sitting down in the pew beside her.

Bea came to join them at that moment. She had been chatting with a few friends. As she took a seat, she said to Thomas, "You must come over to the house afterwards for lunch. Our Sunday wouldn't be complete otherwise."

Thomas smiled. "I would be glad to."

CR

Bea had been telling Betty just the other day how much she had enjoyed the holidays, and Betty sensed that she was feeling somewhat sad now that they were over. Bea loved to host get-togethers and cook, and enjoyed having company in her home.

She was therefore pleased to have Thomas over as a guest for lunch. When they returned home, she went into the kitchen to start preparing a lunch of sandwiches. She insisted that Betty and Thomas relax in the parlor with a cup of tea in the meantime.

They entered the parlor, and were soon joined by Leopold and his toy bird. Betty was glad of the chance to speak with Thomas privately, and to give him the letter.

"Thomas," she began, "A letter came for you yesterday."

Thomas set his cup of tea on the table in front of him, and looked at Betty with curiosity in his eyes. "A letter for me?"

"Yes, it was delivered to The Sapphire Key by a young man who works at the post office sorting mail. He just decided to hand-deliver it."

"Oh," Thomas replied. "That's quite nice, but somewhat out of the ordinary, isn't it?"

Betty shook her head softly. "Not so much out of the ordinary. We've had hand-deliveries of letters before. But this one was very nice, actually." In response to Thomas' inquiring look, she continued, "The young man had never been to a bookstore before, and was so eager to see our books. I let him choose whichever book he wanted, as a gift and a thank you."

Thomas eyes softened and he smiled at her. "He'll be one of your regular customers before you know it."

Betty nodded. Of course, that had been exactly what she

was thinking yesterday. She often felt that they were on the same page about things. It was a nice feeling.

"Well, I'll pick it up tomorrow," he continued, and received a baffled look from Betty.

"Why tomorrow? I didn't leave it at the bookshop. I brought it here for safekeeping."

"Oh," Thomas exclaimed. He had assumed that Betty had indeed left it at The Sapphire Key, though now hearing otherwise, he seemed eager to receive it.

"I'll just go and fetch it," Betty said, and then paused to lower her voice. "Thomas—I think this is *the* letter."

It took him a moment to realize what she meant, and when he did, his eyes widened and he too lowered his voice. "Well, that's wonderful news. Are you sure? It feels like we've been waiting so long for this."

Betty nodded, picking up on Thomas' feeling of disbelief. "Give me just a moment; I'll be right back." Her step was quick as she fetched the letter and brought it to Thomas, who sat waiting and petting Leopold. The cat had jumped up onto the sofa to be next to Thomas, and to be part of their conversation.

As Betty handed it to him, there was a feeling of anticipation that hung in the air. Thomas gently held the envelope in his hands, studying the postmark just as Betty had done. When he looked back up at her, there was a note of wonderment, and also hesitancy, in his eyes. He wanted to open the letter, as she could tell, though a slight apprehension stalled him. She wondered if it was because he wanted to read it in private.

"I think you're right," he breathed. "It's postmarked Gate, Oklahoma. That must mean that this is it."

"Do you want me to..." Betty began to reply.

Thomas immediately said, "I want you to stay. We'll read

it together—please."

Betty was glad to hear him say this. They were both on this journey, and the secret of May Bell Sebastian had become just as important to her as it was to Thomas. Before she could respond, Bea called them into the kitchen.

Feeling the moment start to fade, Thomas cast a look of gratitude towards Betty before slipping the still-unopened envelope into his vest pocket. They would not say anything about it to Bea, and would enjoy their lunch as much as possible while waiting for the next moment to unveil the letter.

Chapter 14

Making Plans

The moment arrived after lunch. Bea again offered the parlor to Thomas and Betty to chat, while she took the rest of the afternoon to work on some correspondence she had not gotten to over the holidays. Betty found this circumstance to be perfect. Little did Bea know, they would all be reviewing correspondence that afternoon.

Sitting across from one another in the parlor, Thomas swiftly opened the envelope and then carefully took out the piece of paper that lay folded inside it. There was a moment where he hesitated, wondering at all of the things that the letter could contain and also all of the things that it may *not* contain. He opened the letter and revealed a page of slanted handwriting that began, *"Dear Mr. Erwinshire..."*

Mrs. Sarah Mitchell Mount
Gate, Oklahoma
January 3, 1921

Dear Mr. Erwinshire,

I received your letter, and my sister Alice had mentioned she knew you. I will try to answer your questions.
Yes, it is true that I knew your mother. She was a dear friend and lovely woman, and she was a writer. It was a long time ago, perhaps 20 years or more, that an accident happened. There was a terrible carriage crash, and your mother and her husband, Phillip, were killed. Their carriage overturned and rolled down a steep hill, finally stopping at the bottom of the

hill near a creek. No one in the carriage survived. At least,
that's what was reported in the papers.
The odd thing is that, two days after the accident when the
bodies were identified, everyone was accounted for except for
your mother's husband. It seems that he was in the carriage,
and then he wasn't. No one could find him. There were men
who went down the hill to look for his body, but it was never
found. Some odd stories came about, a year after the accident,
that he was seen wandering around Seattle, Washington.
Now, I don't know what to make of that, and I have nothing
to say about it. Phillip died in that accident, and that's
the last anyone heard of him. Truth be told, I did not know
this man well, and I was surprised when May married him.
But that's just my opinion.
Your mother is buried in a small cemetery in Kansas. Her
passing was hard, you understand—to lose a young woman
with such promise is unthinkable. We were friends in those
days, and stayed in touch after she married Phillip.
I remember when she had you—she was so happy to have a
baby. So, I'm glad to hear from you, and to know that her
child grew up to be a fine young man. Alice told me you're in
the publishing business.
I hope this helps you to understand what happened to your
parents.

Sincerely,
*   Sarah Mount.*

In the moment after they both finished reading the letter,
the silence in the room was so thick that one could hear a pin
drop. They were speechless as they took in Sarah Mount's
words.

This was Thomas' history, and so Betty felt that it was only right to allow Thomas as much time as he needed to consider everything he learned from the letter. She sat quietly while he skimmed through it again, the only sound in the room being the crinkle of the paper as he held it in his hand. Even Leopold had grown silent and sat on the rug in front of the fireplace, his green eyes fixed on Thomas. He seemed to know that this was an important moment for Thomas.

Eventually, Thomas lowered the letter again and brought his eyes to meet Betty's. There was change in them: a flicker of puzzlement coupled with determination. She waited for him to break the silence.

"So, it's true," he began. "That story you heard, all those months ago, during tea at the Highleys."

Betty started to speak. She realized how dry her mouth had become, and cleared her throat. "You mean, what Mrs. Highley and her niece said about 'Thomas E. and the carriage accident.'"

A few months ago, Betty had attended a tea hosted by Mrs. Highley. At the time, her niece, May Mount (and Sarah Mount's daughter) had been visiting. During the tea, Betty had mentioned Thomas, and that started a conversation about a mysterious "Thomas E." and a carriage accident. Later on, Thomas and Betty had realized that the story might have some truth. It appeared now that the truth had found them in this letter.

Thomas nodded. "I'm not as upset about this letter as I thought I would be. I'm more concerned that I didn't know the truth before now."

Betty softened her gaze, and leaned forward to whisper, "That's not your fault, Thomas."

He closed his eyes briefly, and muttered, "I know. But it

feels like someone's fault. My father—this man, Phillip, who Sarah Mount doesn't seem to know—or my Aunt Violet." A flash of anger appeared on his face. "It seems incredible that Violet didn't know what happened to my mother and father, or has simply been keeping it from me. What would be her reason for not sharing this story?"

Betty knew that Thomas' relationship with his aunt was strained, at best, and she had a feeling that Thomas would find it difficult to ever repair that relationship—especially now. She also had been expecting Thomas to have some kind of reaction to the letter, even if that was to give blame. It was part of the process. He had never really grieved his mother, not properly. Betty hoped that, whatever else it provided, the letter shed some light on his questions and gave him a chance to remember May Bell like Sarah Mount remembered her. It might take him time to process his reaction and feelings, Betty knew, and she was willing to be patient.

"I am glad to have this information, though," Thomas continued, after a few moments of reflection. "It's nice to know that someone *knew* her."

Betty nodded, "Yes, I agree. It sounds as though Sarah and your mother were close for a while."

"And, it sounds like they were in touch before the accident," Thomas added. His demeanor softened again, and he said, "I'm glad that she has visited her gravesite."

Betty felt a tear against her cheek and reached up to brush it away. Yes, it was heartening to know that Sarah made an effort to visit May Bell's gravesite. It reminded her of the visits she and her mother made to Henry's final resting place.

"Betty…" he murmured, after another moment. His expression had shifted again, and he looked as though he was contemplating something. "Betty," he resumed again, as if trying to find the right words.

"Yes, Thomas," she responded warmly, in encouragement.

He looked at her and extended his hand to her, as though he wanted her to take it. She placed her hand in his, and he grasped it. The gesture seemed to give him the courage to say what he said next.

"What would you say if I was to tell you that I wanted to visit my mother's grave?"

Betty's eyes softened, and she answered, "I would say that I understand, and I support you."

He gave her a slight smile, and then swallowed. She could tell that he wanted to say something else. "And…and what would you say if I asked you to come with me?"

Betty was quiet for a moment, and then she said, "I would first ask if you were sure."

"I am," Thomas interjected.

"Then," Betty continued, feeling her heart lifting, "I would say, if you're sure, then I am sure too." After a brief pause, Betty continued, "I would say yes."

In a flash, they both rose to their feet and Thomas pulled Betty towards him in an embrace. In that moment, it felt that the world had shifted and realigned to make sense of things that did not make sense before.

෪

A number of things had changed in January of 1921, though many things had stayed true and remained the same, like friendships and good company. It was a time of new beginnings, and a time for making plans. The future was full of possibilities and opportunities for Betty Featherwin, starting with an impending journey to the midwest to revisit Thomas' past and discover the secret of his parentage. She encouraged Thomas to talk with Mrs. Highley and share his plans. When he did, Mrs. Highley was glad to hear that he planned to make the trip, and mentioned that her sister, Sarah, often received guests and would likely have extra rooms to accommodate him. She also mentioned that her niece, May Mount (who resided in Kansas), would be happy to offer accommodations as well. This was great news, and Thomas and Betty were excited as they began planning for the trip.

Betty was quite used to secrets, and had several of her own: her unfortunate first name, her extraordinary ability to understand her cat, and recently, her discovery of the true value of the sapphire lamps in her bookshop. The secret of Thomas' parentage was the secret that she and Thomas shared together.

It is now the time, she felt, for secrets to be revealed.

The End

Afterword

While this book is a work of fiction, and the scenes, characters and events are a product of my imagination, the setting and historical references throughout the book are based in reality. Coos County, where this story takes place, is a real-life region on the southern coast of Oregon. Locales like the North Bend Mill & Lumber Company, the pier, and the estate of Louis J. Simpson, did, in fact, exist in 1920. The paper dixie cup, the REO fire engine, and myrtle wood figurines are a few historical relics that weave throughout this story. A few of my distant family members found their way to Coos County in the 1800s and 1900s, and worked on the railroad and at the shipyard, which were booming industries during that time. It was an interesting, rich life for them. There was so much newness coming into the world—the telephone, advances in transportation, and changes in the political and social atmosphere—but the area retained its history and charm. As an homage to them, and to that captivating time, I drew from this historical setting to create the world of Betty Featherwin, her friends, and her family.

Also by Sarah Jane Gross

THE TWO SECRECTS

It was 1920 in Coos County, Oregon. Heavy fog was rolling in as Betty Featherwin walked past the pier to the bookshop she inherited from her father. It was a town rich in history and captivation. Her life unfolds in the early years of this coastal area.

Fiction/Literature/ 978-1-7351955-0-6

Coming Soon...

SECRETS REVEALED

In this third installment, the journey continues in the year 1921, with many developments in Coos County, Oregon and elsewhere. Join Betty Featherwin and Thomas Erwinshire as the history and secrets in their lives unfold.

About the Author

Sarah Jane Gross is an author, lawyer, and mediator. She has spent a good portion of her life on a college campus. After graduating from high school, she lived on campus at the University of California, Davis in northern California, where she graduated with a Bachelor's in English and Expository Writing. After graduation, she stayed on to receive a teaching credential and Master's in Education and, for a while, taught middle school and high school English. She then pursued further education, and attended Chapman University School of Law in southern California, where she graduated with a law degree. After passing the Bar exam, she worked for a firm practicing education law. She then decided to focus on a different area of law, and was accepted to Pepperdine University School of Law in the coastal city of Malibu, California in Los Angeles County. She lived on campus and graduated with a Master's in Law through the Straus Institute for Dispute Resolution. She returned to

Orange County, where she spearheaded a pilot program in eldercaring coordination for the courts. She continues to advocate for court-connected programs to address the needs of elders and their families, including mediation programs. Sarah has had many legal articles published, and enjoys creative writing, which has always been a passion for her.

☙❧